RED CLAY

True Stories of
Life in the Rural South

By

MYLDRED FLANIGAN HUTCHINS
Illustrated by John Kollock

Cherokee Publishing Company
Atlanta, Georgia
1988

Library of Congress Cataloging-in-Publication Data

Hutchins, Myldred Flanigan, 1908-
    Red clay : true stories about people who lived in and around the
small town of Auburn, Georgia / by Myldred Flanigan Hutchins.
        p.   cm.
    Reprint. Originally published: Lakemont, Ga. : Copple House
Books, c1981.
    ISBN 0-87797-075-0 (pbk. : alk. paper) : $5.95
    1. Auburn Region (Ga.)--Social life and customs--Anecdotes.
2. City and town life--Georgia--Auburn Region--Anecdotes.
I. Title.
F294.A895H87 1988   88-17794
975.8'195--dc19   CIP

Copyright © 1981 by Myldred F. Hutchins

This book is printed on acid-free paper which conforms to the
American National Standard Z39.48-1984 *Permanence of Paper for
Printed Library Materials.* Paper that conforms to this standard's
requirements for pH, alkaline reserve and freedom from
groundwood is anticipated to last several hundred years without
significant deterioration under normal library use and storage
conditions. ⊗

Manufactured in the United States of America

ISBN: 0-87797-075-0
(Previously ISBN: 0-932298-13-3)
97 96 95 94 93 92 91 90   10 9 8 7 6 5 4 3 2 1

Cherokee Publishing Company is an operating division of
The Larlin Corporation, P.O. Box 1730, Marietta, GA 30061

CONTENTS

Red Clay — Poem   9

Chapter 1
Pros and Cons of Country Living: From How to
Take a Country Bath to Using Finger Bowls   11

Chapter 2
A Town Springs Up Out of Red Clay, and
What Made It Grow   20

Chapter 3
The Church Was the Hub, and the Wheel of
Social Life Spun Around It.   36

Chapter 4
Come On, Let's Go to "Big Meetin' "   49

Chapter 5
From College to the 'Tater Patch —
Perry-Rainey College   59

Chapter 6
Christmas, County Style   71

Chapter 7
Family Life Patterns   78

Chapter 8
Tied Down to a General Store   98

Chapter 9
Tom Foolery, Experiences in a Hospital Ward,
and Name Collecting   110

Chapter 10
The Early Depression Years — Penniless but
Having Fun   126

RED CLAY

The road scrape levels the bank beside the road, removing
    the grass and weeds,
Revealing the smooth crimson loveliness of Georgia clay.
Drops of moisture in the soil sparkle as the sun's rays
    touch the droplets,
Making them look like jewels against the crimson, velvety
    clay.

But Georgia's clay can be treacherous when wet. Auto-
    mobile tires, on an unpaved road
Slip and slide as on ice. An unsuspecting driver can end up
    in a ditch where tires spin
Digging deeper and deeper into the red mud
    until hopelessly stuck.

When summer's burning sun touches Georgia's red clay and
    robs it of its moisture
The clay takes on the color of dried brick, and deep cracks
    appear on its surface.
It becomes dry and brittle. Finally it is a fine dust
    covering everything in a powdery red shroud.

Winter, too, can bring drastic changes to Georgia's red clay.
Cold dry weather brings the baked-clay appearance. But
    let rains come with freezing cold, and ice crystals
Spring from its surface in irregular patterns. The ground
    takes on a honeycomb appearance.

Georgia's red clay has special qualities—unusual ones.
The Indians discovered some red clays were suitable for
    dyeing cloth.
Early white settlers learned from Indians that Auburn
    had such a clay bank.
Strange that all red clay can not be used for dyeing.

Durable red brick can be made from Georiga's red clay.
Auburn's first brick store was built from local brick—
    a product of Auburn's red clay.
It stands after 75 years, testifying to another use
    for our practical red clay.

However bold, bleak, and bare Georgia's red hills may
    appear,
Crops flourish and prosper in her clay. I stand in awe of
    the way man is tested and threatened
By this beautiful and temperamental soil.

The Red Hills cry, "Use me." Yet the sticky mud
    entraps one, and the powdery red dust forms a blanket
That defies both broom and mop. But freshly turned soil
    reveals
A crimson and velvety beauty that words can not define.
Georgia's Red Clay, I salute YOU!

Chapter I

PROS AND CONS OF COUNTRY LIVING: FROM HOW TO TAKE A COUNTRY BATH TO USING FINGER BOWLS

Growing up in a small town, from 1910 to 1927, had advantages and disadvantages. In retrospect the advantages outweighed the disadvantages.

Life was simple and uncomplicated. As long as there were food, clothes, and a house to live in our basic needs were met. Anything above this was considered a luxury. Life centered around our home, our school, and our church. Without radio, T.V., movies, paved roads, and the automobile, we learned to depend upon our own initiative for entertainment and amusement.

The disadvantages did not become apparent until one was removed from his home environment. I remember the first electric fan I ever saw. My father's bachelor brother was getting married to a lady in Winder. It was to be a home wedding, and my family went to Atlanta, by train, to buy new clothes to wear to the wedding. I remember my dress quite well. It was white with a square neck, insets of lace, and tiny tucks, and it cost eight dollars, wholesale!

The day of the wedding came. It was to be an evening ceremony. We drove there in the family Maxwell. I was the only child there, and I'm not sure that I was invited. The only thing I remember about the wedding was seeing my future aunt, in a white dress with a long train, descending the curving staircase with her father. At the foot of the stairs where my uncle waited, she took his arm and they walked to an altar in an adjoining room. He must have been trembling for she gave his arm a shake which was exactly what he needed, for he straightened up and they walked proudly to the altar!

But to get back to the electric fan. The reception was held at the home of another uncle. When we arrived, all the ladies were told they could go upstairs to freshen up. That was not my first introduction to an indoor bathroom, I'd seen them in Atlanta. This aunt and uncle were not at all happy to see a child at a wedding reception, so my parents told me to stay upstairs.

To amuse myself I walked around and looked. The only thing I remember seeing was something that had to be a fan because it cooled me. It was on a dresser in the bed-room where the ladies went to powder their noses and smooth their hair. I was fascinated! It turned, making a whirring noise. I stood there as if hypnotized. I did not know it was powered by electricity, but did want to know what made it go. I also wanted to know if I could slow it down, or maybe stop it, so I stuck my finger in! It is a wonder my finger was not cut off, but I jerked it out in a big hurry. It hurt terribly, but I did not cry—I was afraid to, for I knew I'd done something I should not have done. I still didn't know what made the thing go.

When my mother came upstairs for me, I asked what it was, and she told me it was an electric fan, and that electricity also made the lights burn. We had oil lamps at home. I was simply out of my home environment, and everything was strange.

I was soon to learn more about the strange ways of city life. My father had a general store in Auburn, and I was sometimes allowed to go with him and my mother to Atlanta, by train, to buy goods for the store.

My father always ate at Peacock Alley. I guess it was the only restaurant he knew. A salesman from a wholesale house must have taken him there for lunch at some time. I'm sure Peacock Alley was on Peachtree or Whitehall, not far from the wholesale district, for it was only a short walk to reach it. It seems to me we had to climb stairs to reach the restaurant.

I had never seen a place as beautiful as Peacock Alley! I was quite overwhelmed by the pompous waiters in uniforms. I'd never heard of a menu, and when my father asked what I wanted to eat I said, "Ham and eggs." It was all I could think of. I remember nothing about the food, but when our plates were removed, and a little bowl of water and a fresh napkin were placed before us I didn't have the slightest idea why it was there! I was told it was a "finger bowl." I was delighted, and enjoyed using it immensely. Sometime later I ate in a restaurant that did *not* have finger bowls, so I asked for one, but did not get it; so I improvised by simply dipping my napkin in my water glass and wiping my fingers with it.

To those who had never ridden a train nor been to Atlanta, a trip there seemed like going to a distant land. Three teenaged boys who grew up several miles from Auburn, saved their money to take a train ride to Atlanta. This was a day's excursion for them and they were elated at having this adventure. They boarded the train at Carl, a flag-station one mile from Auburn. The boys walked through the train and were on the rear platform when it reached Auburn. People always came out to see a train go by, so the boys waved to everyone as they passed through town. As it pulled out of the station, after a brief stop, one of the boys took off his cap, waved to the people and shouted, "We're off to Atlanta, good-bye ole Georgia." What a difference the automobile and paved roads have made in our lives!

It was gratifying later to learn that "city people" had equally as much difficulty coping with life in the country.

A New Use for the Barnyard Pump

We had two city cousins, in their early twenties, who came to see my sister every summer, and stayed a week. I could never figure out why they came because they missed the comforts of an indoor bathroom so much—but they did like to eat! A tub bath was the thing they seemed to miss most of all, and they devised a way to bathe that somewhat shocked us. We had a pump in what had been the well shelter, near the barn. The top of the well had been covered with a wide board when the pump was installed. The cousins decided this could be used as a shower. One would lie down on the wide board, and the other would pump water. Of course, the bather hung off the board from her knees down, but the water splashed and trickled down nicely: We were too modest to try such

bathing procedures, even under cover of darkness, but they had no hesitancy about disrobing at the well-shelter. I guess we were thinking about that occasional person who might walk by, as the side walk was a few feet away. The only light came from the house or from trains that might come by — and those headlights could be mighty bright! In our small town a "lady" simply did not undress in the yard and take a bath, even in the dark.

Bathing, Country Style

The problems of bathing in the country reminds me of another story about "city people." One family had some city relatives come in unexpectedly one afternoon and announce they were spending the night, and were looking forward to some fresh vegetables, and "good ole fried chicken."

The family was in a state of confusion, as they rushed around preparing the evening meal, and making arrangements for additional sleeping space, as they had only one guest room. The younger members of the family complained that they were having to be servants to that bunch of "city dudes.' sitting on the front porch, rocking!

The teen-aged daughter of the city relatives had never been in a house that did not have a bathroom, and this created problems. At the table that night she persisted in continuing the discussion of how one could take a bath without a bathroom. Finally, she asked, "How in the world can you take a bath without a bathtub?" The oldest "country cousin" answered "You get a bowl of water and a bath cloth. You wash down as far as possible, and up as far as possible, and then wash possible itself." No one even smiled, but that ended the discussion. The daughter who had given the instructions for taking a country bath did not get scolded by her parents. I guess they were tired of all the questions, too. By the way, the city cousin ate so much blackberry pie she was sick!

Years later, when I was in college at Emory, I frequently brought friends home for the weekend. I was one of three Freshman girls who entered Emory my first year, and I rode a local train back and forth each day. The first time I brought Mary home with me she was very self-conscious about showing her ignorance of country life. In private she asked me many questions, and was serious about the whole matter. She asked me how we could tell a rooster from a hen, because she had never seen a live chicken!

She Was Merely a Phi Beta Kappa

Mary visited me for a number of years and came in for much teasing, because of her ignorance of country life. She graduated Phi Beta Kappa from Emory, and went on to teach in a small Middle-Georgia town.

Dutifully she went to church her first Sunday in town, and was asked to read the Scripture lesson in Sunday

School. Obligingly, she rose to read and saw a proper name she had never seen before. There were no diacritical marks or pronunciation guide to help her. Had she been accustomed to the "fire and brimstone" type of preaching that was common in small towns, she would have known how to pronounce that word! But she was merely a Phi Beta Kappa, so Beelzebub came out Bezelbub, amid many smiles and a few giggles! She knew she had mispronounced the word, and sat there mortified that she had done such a thing on her first Sunday in town, when she had been so anxious to make a good impression.

After service a young man introduced himself, and asked to walk her to her boarding house. He was "so nice" and friendly that she decided to ask him how she should have pronounced that word and he told her. They became friends and later married. But about country life Mary still had a lot to learn.

The young man owned a cattle farm. The following summer Mary visited me. She told us about the fine thoroughbred cattle Joe raised. We asked what breed he raised and she replied, "They have red bodies and white faces, and are called Heifers." Of course, she meant Herefords! She did not know heifers were young female cows. I'm afraid we never ceased teasing her about the new breed of cows Joe raised.

When in college I sometimes felt I had been cheated out of a great deal by having grown up in a little town. Yet, college classmates loved to come home with me for weekends, and seemed to think our parties and social events were more fun than anything they had experienced.

After college, I was in Auburn only for visits. When I married my husband's work required that we move frequently, and it was with a sense of relief, after the birth of our daughter, Anne, that we decided to come back to Auburn and settle down. We stayed there about nine years, and Anne enjoyed the good experiences of living in a small town. These little stories illustrate some of the things she experienced while living there.

What is Tomorrow?

Children can sometimes surprise adults with their understanding. Anne and her little playmate, Dolly Size-more, were visiting my sister, Mrs. Tom Ethridge. They were playing in her yard when she heard them discussing their first week of school. It seemed that things had gone pretty well, but Dolly was puzzled about one thing. She said, "My teacher is always talking about tomorrow, and I don't understand what tomorrow is." Anne thought a minute and said, "Well, Dolly, I think it is like this—right now is today, yesterday was an old today, and tomorrow is a brand new today."

Flashlight Bugs

Anne was about three years old, and having the time of her life chasing lightning bugs around the lawn. Her grand-father called, "What kind of bugs are those, Anne?" She replied, "Why, don't you know? They are flashlight bugs." Now, our little granddaughter, having heard this story, laughs and says, "Mother's flashlight bugs!"

Earbobs, What Else?

At two and one-half years, Anne was seeing her first baby calf. Her Uncle Tom had taken her out to the barn to see the calf. In answer to questions she was saying in her baby way, "These are her ears, these are her eyes, her nose, her mouth." Then she discovered the tiny little horns almost hidden in tufts of hair. Her puzzled expression suddenly gave way to delight as she exclaimed, "These are—these are her earbobs."

We moved back to Atlanta where my husband worked with the Georgia Bureau of Investigation and later helped organize the State Police Academy. Living near Emory, Anne attended Druid Hills High School and later Emory University, but we all have fond memories of life in a small town.

Chapter 2

A TOWN SPRINGS UP OUT OF RED CLAY,
AND WHAT MADE IT GROW

Old Auburn

There was an Auburn post office long before Auburn became a town. Every little settlement seemed to have a store, a church, and usually a school house. The storekeeper served as postmaster, and a section of his store was set aside for that purpose. Auburn was in Gwinnett County until 1914, when it became part of the new county of Barrow. Gwinnett County records show there was an Auburn post office as early as 1837, and its location was near Appalachee Baptist Church, which is still an active church.

This early settlement was named for the Red Clay that abounds in that area. The Indians told early white settlers there was a certain red clay bank in the vicinity, of the future town of Auburn, where they dug red clay and used it for dyeing cloth.

Auburn's Red Clay

A cousin of mine, the late Russell Bradley, told of his experience with Auburn's red clay. As a boy, Russell lived several miles from town. One cold winter morning, his mother gave him a sack, told him to saddle the mule, go to Auburn and fill the sack with "the special red mud," so she could dye the cloth she had been weaving. He knew the exact place where the mud was to be found, for he had gone with his mother several times to get clay for dyeing cloth.

He was just a youngster, and was not at all keen about taking this long cold ride to Auburn. As he went along, he looked at the banks of red clay he passed. This clay looked just like the clay he had seen his mother get in Auburn, so he decided to shorten his trip, and get clay from the roadside instead of going into town. He dug into the clay bank and filled his sack. Back home all went well until his mother tried to the use the clay for her dyeing. The color would not hold! Now, Russell was in trouble. When confronted by his mother he had to admit the clay had not come from the special red clay bank in Auburn, but from the roadside.

Auburn Incorporated

With the coming of the Seaboard Railroad in 1891, people began moving to be near the railroad, a means of communication and transportation. The town of Auburn grew up along each side of the railroad tracks and was incorporated in 1892. The railroad had a plat of the town drawn and the land surveyed. Trees and street lights lined the streets on each side of the railroad.

Reminiscent of Robert Louis Stevenson's poem, "The Old Lamplighter," is the whimsical story my sister, the late Mrs. Tom Ethridge, used to tell. When our father first moved to Auburn from Hoschton, the family lived in the two-story white house directly across the railroad from my father's store. (Durden Enterprises now occupies the store.) As a child, my sister watched for the policeman to come by late in the afternoon, carrying a short ladder, to light the street lamps. When the lamps needed refilling he carried a can of kerosene oil to replenish them.

Trees and Street Lights Vanish

She also recalled the fate of the street lights and the beautiful young trees that had been planted along the streets. This was a sinister tale of "gradual disappearance."

The town folk were amazed one Monday morning to see that some of the trees were gone from the streets. It was the talk of the town. What had become of the trees? How could they have disappeared overnight? A few weeks later more of the trees and a few of the street lights were missing. Over a period of months all the trees and street lights that could be easily pulled up had vanished.

Finally, the great mystery was solved. The missing trees and lights were discovered a few miles from town in an almost-dry lake. The owner of the land found them when a long drought caused the water in the lake to recede. He had a good idea who was responsible! He confronted some boys whom he knew ran together on weekends and roamed the countryside playing pranks and getting into trouble. The boys confessed and said it had been great fun listening to the citizens of Auburn talk as they speculated on what could have happened to the trees and street lights. The names of these boys reads like a "Who's Who" of future prominent citizens of the area! My sister knew most of them. Who longs for the good ole days, before the days of vandalism?

Carl vs. Auburn

A great deal of animosity existed between the towns of Auburn and Carl. Carl was one mile from Auburn, and both towns wanted the railroad station. Auburn won in this battle over the station because two Auburn citizens gave the right-of-way for the station, and Carl became a flag station. But the hard feelings between the two towns continued. The resentment extended to the young people. The Carl boys told Auburn boys that Carl girls were off-limits to them, and they would be rocked every time they were caught dating a Carl girl. This warning did not stop the Auburn boys from dating Carl girls, but quite a few were rocked and had to out-run the Carl boys.

My father's brother, Dilmus, had the misfortune of being caught one Sunday night as he walked home from a date. He was surrounded before he realized anyone was following him. He was told to dance; when he refused a pistol was fired into the ground near his feet. Again he was instructed to dance, and he did. He said he figured it was safer to dance than to be shot! After he had danced they let him go. He said that was the last date he had in Carl.

Tramps

My mother told of tramps who followed the railroad tracks. They usually slept under the floor of the warehouses near the station, but if the weather was cold, they tried to get inside the warehouses to sleep on the cotton seed stored there.

Begging for food was common. A tramp would go to the back door and ask for a meal, usually breakfast or dinner. They seldom offered to work to pay for food. People did not seem afraid of them, and they harmed no one.

Although some families refused to give tramps food, my mother was a soft-touch and never refused anyone. She asked a tramp one day why so many came to her door. He answered that tramps marked trees in front of a house where food was given. He invited her to go with him to the front of the house, and there he showed her the marked tree. It had many little verticle marks where tramps had left their calling cards!

Gypsy Horse Traders

There was, however, a group of wandering people that the town folk were afraid of—the gypsy horse traders.

They traveled in covered wagons and later in cars, and came to town twice each year, spring and fall. They camped about a mile from town, not far from Appalachee church, in a wooded area. The women sold lace and other handmade articles from door to door. Young children accompanied them, and they darted into a house as soon as a door was opened. The children wandered through the house while the women engaged the lady of the house in conversation. You dared not leave the door or else the women would come into the house, too. The children picked up small articles and food, and left by whatever door was handy. We always kept our screen doors fastened if gypsies were in town.

Groups of women and children often descended on the stores in town, pretending to want to purchase something. They were everywhere, going behind counters and picking up anything that interested them. My father said they could steal with you looking at them.

The young gypsy women were pretty and great flirts. They wore full skirts and blouses with bright scarves tied around their heads, and lots of beads and bracelets. In passing a store where men were sitting in front, it was not unusual for a gypsy girl to sit down in some man's lap. She might tousle his hair and chuck him under the chin, but her hands always found their way into his pockets. These were usually older men, and they never heard the end of the teasing after such an experience.

At night, after a day of so-called horse trading, the men built camp fires, and there was singing and dancing. Some of the more venturesome young people in town went and joined in their festivities. The gypsies left as suddenly as they came. When they departed horses and sometimes cows, were missing in the community.

Auburn Messenger

Auburn had a newspaper called the *Auburn Messenger*. I have seen only two copies of this paper. One interesting thing in the July 26, 1901, Vol. i, No. 5 edition, was the listing of Professional Cards by the local doctors. There were three such cards and they appeared on the front page.

The first: "T.A. Fowler, Physician and Surgeon, will answer all calls promptly day or night." Of added interest was this notice: "If you want Ice-Cold Drinks consisting of Lemonade, Milk Shakes, Soda Water, Ginger Ale, and Root Beer, call on: Yours for comfort, Blakey Perry." (In Dr. Fowler's Office)

The second card: "Laugh and grow fat is the axiom. I could commend some of the reliable up-to-date family medicines to you. I have a splended line of patent medicines and will put them to you at living prices. Also will fill prescriptions promptly. Yours in sickness as well as in health, R.B. Moore, M.D."

The third card: "L.P. Pharr, Physician and Surgeon, offers his services to the people of Auburn and surrounding country."

I never knew Dr. Fowler, but one of his daughters was my first Sunday School teacher. I was in the beginners, or card class. She told us about some Biblical character dying, and that was my first introduction to death. I was so frightened I went home and asked my mother when I was going to die. I got up in her lap and cried myself to sleep.

Dr. Fowler's youngest son was named W.C. He, with two other youngsters, all around seven years of age, were riding with Squire Hawthorne, Justice of the Peace, in his buggy. Mr. Hawthorne asked the boys if they had ever seen anyone get married. He hastened to add that if they would come to Sunday School early the next day, they could see

him perform a wedding ceremony. Two of the boys said
they had never seen anyone get married. W.C. said nothing,
and Mr. Hawthorne asked, "Well, have you ever seen
anyone get married?" W.C. replied, "Noboby but my
grandma." It was true, his grandmother, a widow, had
recently been married!

Another son, Winton Fowler, liked to tease one of his
sisters about her big mouth. He would say there was one
thing that God could not do, and that naturally provoked
the question, "What can't God do?" "Make Villie's mouth
bigger without moving her ears." She and my sister were
close friends, and I was fond of her and resented his
teasing, although she accepted it with good grace.

Dr. R.B. Moore told this story about how he cured
Aunt Nancy Chandler of a strange ailment.

Aunt Nancy and the Spring Lizard

Aunt Nancy and Uncle John Chandler had been slaves
in their youth. Aunt Nancy, small and almost white in
color, was proud and had a haughty demeanor. Uncle John,
a kind and stately old gentleman, was liked by everyone.
They lived near Auburn in a beautiful little wooded area,
and drank cold spring water from a spring just back of
their house.

One day Aunt Nancy became ill and went to bed. After
a day or so, as she was no better, Uncle John sent for Dr.
Moore. When the good doctor arrived, he asked Aunt
Nancy what was wrong. She replied she had swallowed a
"Spring lizard," and could feel it running around inside
her! After an examination and finding nothing wrong, he
left some medicine that he assured her would take care of
the lizard.

Aunt Nancy did not improve, and Dr. Moore was
called a second time. This time, he stopped by a creek,
caught a spring lizard, and put it in a small jar.

Again he examined Aunt Nancy, and could find nothing wrong. He asked everyone to leave the room, so he could give her a more thorough examination. He asked her to place her hand on the spot where she could feel the lizard. He pressed down firmly on the spot, had her open her mouth and say "Ah." Then, before her astonished eyes, he held up the spring lizard he had caught. He called the family in to see the spring lizard that had caused all the trouble! Aunt Nancy had a speedy recovery. And we say psychological medicine is a recent phenomenon!

Stealing the Peach Brandy

Dr. Pharr had an interesting experience with one of his patients. In the Auburn Methodist Church hung a framed list of Lincoln-Lee League signers. I know little about this Lincoln-Lee organization, but the signers had pledged never to drink any alcoholic beverage.

One of the Lincoln-Lee members was a patient of Dr. Pharr's, and she had double pneumonia. Double pneumonia was considered a deadly disease at that time, and she was not expected to live. Dr. Pharr told the family when the fever broke she would need whiskey to help her body withstand the shock. The family explained this would be a problem, because she had signed a pledge NEVER to drink alcohol.

Dr. Pharr talked to his patient, but she still refused to take any kind of alcohol. He then asked if she would consent to take some homemade peach brandy, and he hastened to explain that this was really not alcoholic and tasted almost like pickled peaches. He also assured her she would not be breaking her pledge. Finally, she agreed.

When he emerged from the room he told her family she had consented to take homemade peach brandy. He chuckled as he imparted this information and said that he had stretched the truth a little when he told her brandy was non-alcoholic, but he felt justified in doing it.

The family was concerned as to where they could find peach brandy. Dr. Pharr said he knew where he could get a good quality of homemade peach brandy. They asked where he planned to buy it, he laughed and said it would cost nothing because he planned to steal it! He explained that a cotton buyer in town, who was also a good Baptist deacon in the church a short distance from Auburn, made a high quality peach brandy, and he always had a bottle hidden in his cotton warehouse. The doctor could not offer to buy it, because the deacon would not admit he

made the peach brandy! He would just have to take what
he needed. Dr. Pharr would not reveal how he knew about
the brandy, in the first place, nor how he knew where it
was hidden.

He did get the brandy and his patient lived. I guess
doctors sometimes have to do sneaky things in order to do
what they think is best for their patients.

The Old Red Rooster

Mr. John Wood had a store and a grist mill, and was a
staunch member of the Auburn Baptist Church. He was a
small and lively man who loved a good story. He had a
habit of rubbing his hands together as he talked. One could
tell when he was preparing to tell a story by the way he
rubbed his hands together.

Mr. Wood, as did most of the merchants in town,
bought produce from farm families. On Saturdays families
often came to town with butter, eggs, and chickens to sell
or "trade" for goods the merchant had to sell. Mr. Wood
bought a strangely marked red rooster from a lady one
Saturday morning, and put it in a chicken coop at the rear
of his store.

When he came back from the chicken coop, he noticed
several boys in front of the store. They were whispering
and laughing and he wondered what mischief they were
up to. They continued to hang around the store, and he
determined to watch them, but got busy and forgot all
about the boys.

Some time later he noticed he had another customer
who had a chicken to sell. When he started to take the
chicken, he was startled to see it was the same peculiarly
marked rooster he had bought from the lady. He looked at
his customer closely, and recognized one of the boys who
had been standing in front of his store. He did not let on
that he recognized the boy, but started around the store to

put the rooster back in the coop. The boys had moved from the front to the side of the store, so they could watch him. They giggled when they saw him put the rooster into the coop. He decided it might be fun to go along with them and see what they would do next.

After a while, another one of the boys came in with the same red rooster. Mr. Wood bought the chicken, smiling to himself, he went to the chicken coop for the third time to deposit the red rooster. As he passed the boys they laughed, but he said not a word, it would soon be time to let them know they had not fooled him, after all.

He was waiting for the next boy when he came in with the red rooster. They were now very sure of themselves.

Mr. Wood bought the chicken, and took him back to the chicken coop. As he returned to the store, he stopped by where the boys were standing, "Well, boys, the game is over, I'm tired of carrying that old rooster back to the chicken coop. We have all had some fun and you ought to be full of candy by this time, but I recognized him the first time you brought him in!" The boys stood with mouths wide open and speechless. This time it was Mr. Wood who broke into a loud laugh as he re-entered his store.

People

Thinking back over other people I remember in Auburn, there was the dentist's office right next to Mr. Wood's store. I always stopped and peeped in when I passed by—the sight of the big chair was enough to make one run away. Dr. Truesdale was the dentist. I played with his daughter, but was always afraid of him.

Mr. T.E. Collins had the only soda fountain in town. I was not allowed, as a child, to sit at one of the round tables and order a drink from the fountain, but I could buy an ice cream cone and walk out with it. On Saturdays I went to buy a loaf of bakery bread for Sunday Dinner. It came by train from Atlanta once a week—just in time for the weekend. I don't know why Mr. Collins was the only merchant who carried bakery bread, but it was someting special to have sandwiches made from "store bought" bread for Sunday dinner.

I envied Mr. Collins' son, Jewell, of his little automobile. I was not allowed to have a bike, it was not polite for girls to ride bikes, and I did want something I could ride. Jewell rode up and down the sidewalk in front of their store and home, which was next door, pedalling that car, how I longed to ride in it. Another boy in town, Bertram Cosby, had a goat and wagon. He rode all over town, and sometimes stopped by our house to talk, but I was never asked to ride. Girls were not supposed to want to do the things that boys did.

A grocery store owned by Mr. Jim Mitchell and his wife, was unique. On certain days during the week, Mr. Mitchell hitched his white horse to a covered wagon and went out into the country and sold groceries from door to door, while his wife kept store. It was a big help to those who lived in the country to have the store come to them.

Noah's Ark

Auburn's first liberated woman was Miss Ella Hawthorne, daughter of Squire Hawthorne! She owned a woman's apparel store, and must have been the first to introduce the "layered look" as she always wore a long sleeved dress or blouse, but added little jackets of all kinds. She was a petite lady with her dark hair worn in a braid around her head. She wore wide brimmed hats winter and summer. She never married. It was reported that she was engaged to be married and the date for the wedding set, but she forgot about it and went out of town that day!

Miss Ella was never in a hurry and was very soft spoken. One never knew what time her store would open—it just depended on how many people she stopped to visit with on her way to work. Her store came to be known as Noah's Ark, as she still had some of the first goods she ever bought. The building was chocked full of everything imaginable. Her counters and shelves were piled high, but she had a wonderful memory, and she could tell you, when you inquired about an item, if she had it. If you were patient she would find it eventually.

Mr. Will Ethridge had a grocery store, but I can never remember going in it except before Christmas to buy fresh coconuts, which my mother must have to make her Christmas cakes and candy.

Lila Pool lived on the street back of our house, and we played together almost every day in summer. Her father had a store, and when her mother sent her to the store for something, I often went along. Her father always hugged us and said he was going to bite our ears off—and I believed him for he would nibble on them. Then he would laugh, and go to the candy counter and give us candy.

Another interesting thing about him, that I have never forgotten, was his refusal to pray in public. He was a leader in the community and in the Baptist Church. He served as Sunday School Superintendent, deacon, and teacher of the Adult Bible Class for years. Yet, when called upon to pray in public he would say in a rather high pitched voice, "Excuse me." I never found out why he felt this reluctance to pray in public. But come to think of it, I feel the same way. Praying is to be done in private, as far as I am concerned.

Don't Forget Your Bed Quilt

Mr. George Stewart was a farmer and leader in the Auburn Baptist Church. He never missed a service, and always occupied the same seat in church. One very chilly fall night, we went to services at the Baptist Church. There was no fire built in the stove, and we were all shivering. Many of the windowpanes were broken and the wind whizzed through these broken windows. Panes were frequently broken in summer when windows were opened and not supported by window sticks. They often came down with a crash, and glass fell all over the floor. It was quite expensive to repair them when cold weather came.

We all shivered through the service, and someone called the church into business session, after the sermon was over, to discuss repairing the windows and making arrangements for fires to be built in the stove before services. Mr. Stewart made a timely comment that became a favorite

saying in our family during cold weather. He said something "besides talk" had to be done about heating that
church or he was going to start bringing a bed quilt with
him to wrap up in, because he was about to freeze! We
agreed with him 100 percent, and after that when we
started to church in winter, we would say, "Don't forget
your bed quilt." Pot-bellied stoves were not adequate to
heat any building comfortably in winter unless a fire was
built *well in advance* of a meeting.

In trying to summarize Auburn's early history, I would
have to say the Seaboard Railroad was responsible for its
birth and growth. It did become a prosperous little town.
There were cotton warehouses, cotton gins, sawmills,
grist mills, livery stables, barber shops, restaurants, boarding
houses, numerous stores, a bank, and a newspaper. My
father had salesmen on the road selling organs, sewing
machines, and lightning rods. He also shipped mineral
water from Flanigan's Mineral Springs, located several
miles from town. The water was shipped by train, in 5 and
10 gallon jugs, fitted into individual wooden crates. The
crates were made especially for that purpose, so the large
jugs would not be difficult to handle. This mineral spring
was a favorite place to picnic. It was in a deep wooded
area, cool and pleasant even in the hottest weather, and
the water was ice cold.

Chapter 3

THE CHURCH WAS THE HUB, AND THE WHEEL
OF SOCIAL LIFE SPUN AROUND IT

The church was a social as well as a religious institu-
tion. We had a Baptist, a Methodist, and later a Christian
church. There was Sunday School each Sunday, and
preaching services once a month at each church. The Baptist and Christian Sunday Schools were held in the
morning, and the Methodist in the afternoon. Sunday was
a full day, as most people attended Sunday School in the
morning and again in the afternoon. Church services were
held on different Sundays in the month, so there was only
one Sunday without church services to attend—except an
occasional fifth Sunday. There was nowhere else to go, so
these full Sunday schedules were appreciated and taken
advantage of by old and young.

Dating couples had a heyday on Sunday, but were well

chaperoned, because a crowd of their friends were always around. Young people went as a group in those days, and they loved to walk. In spring, they walked to Parks' Mill, or to what was called "The Rocks," to gather wild honeysuckle (azaleas), crabapple blossoms, and mountain laurel. The Mill was about 1½ miles from Auburn, and the Rocks about ½ mile. In summer, if the weather was not too hot, they walked to Carl, or the tressle near Appalachee Baptist Church. When it was really hot they went to someone's home, and perhaps had a watermelon cutting, ate fresh peaches or grapes, and sometimes made ice cream. In the fall the long walks continued, and sometimes the group went home with Tom and Loy Ethridge to pick chinquains (much like chestnuts, but smaller). On the way home they played "Jack in the Bush"—guessing how many chinquapins one held in his hand. In winter, when it was not possible to go walking, they met in homes and had "singings" or just talked. The art of conversation was well developed at that time. Our home was right behind the Methodist church, and seemed to be a favorite place for the young people to gather. On this particular Sunday, the crowd had arrived, and I eagerly rushed in. I was not old enough to go to school, but my sister was of dating age. I lisped and the young people liked to tease me just to hear me talk, and I was not at all shy—I really think I was a brat, hopefully due to too much attention. This little story might be entitled—

She Knew Her Bible

I marched into the room and sat on the round piano stool, and enjoyed its merry-go-round effect. I loved the attention I was given, and readily answered all the questions asked me, and many times volunteered information not asked for.

One boy asked, "Your sister has a new boyfriend,

doesn't she?'' I nodded my head with a knowing smile.
Someone else asked how I liked him. I replied I didn't
like him at all. Of course, the next question was Why I
didn't like him. I glibly answered, "He's too hairy. He has
black hairs all over his arms and hands, and when he asked
me to sit on his lap, I couldn't stand for him to touch
me. Why, he's just like Esau in the Bible."

My sister got me out of the room before the laughter
subsided, and any more questions could be asked. You see,
the brother of the hairy one was sitting there.

Sitting up 'til bedtime with friends, was something
families enjoyed any time of the week. Everyone ate supper early, so as to get dishes washed before dark. It was a
bother to carry lamps from room to room. Children loved
this kind of visiting. When the weather was warm they
could go out and play, and in winter they could pop corn,
or play games over in the corner away from the grown-
ups.

Spending the day was another common custom on Sundays. Families were usually invited in advance, and there was much hustle and bustle on Saturday getting food ready. It was understood that the "spend the day party" would follow Sunday School and Church. The following story is an example of what strange customs one might encounter when visiting friends.

How to Keep the Corn Bread Warm

This particular family had never visited in the home of their hosts before. Both families attended Sunday School and church services. It was a cold winter day, and everyone was hungry. Their hosts had been talking about the fresh turnip greens and hot corn bread they would enjoy. They had assured the guests it would take only a few minutes to get the food on the table.

The guests were invited into the master bedroom where the only fire was burning. The two ladies went to the kitchen to get the food on the table, while everyone else sat around the open fire. Soon the hostess came into the bedroom, went to the bed, raised the covers at the foot of the bed and withdrew a towel-wrapped object. She said, "This is the way I keep my corn bread warm. While it is steaming hot, I wrap it in a towel, and put it at the foot of the bed where our feet have been. There is nothing like a feather-bed to hold the heat, and the moisture from our feet keeps it from drying out." Somehow the visitors seemed to lose their appetite for fresh turnip greens and HOT CORN BREAD.

Showing Off On a Bicycle

The family lived about a mile from Auburn; a large family of boys and only one girl. It was summer and the daughter was having a spend-the-day party for some of her girl friends.

The girls had been quite conscious of the brothers as they went in and out of the house. Well aware of the girls' presence, the brothers had tried to "show off" on several occasions.

One of the boys had a new bicycle. He had gone to town for his mother, and as he came in sight of the front porch where the girls were sitting he decided he would do a little fancy riding to impress them.

The two-story house was large with a porch extending across the front. Boxwood grew along the walk leading to the porch. The walk was covered in beautiful white sand. Little did he know how treacherous sand can be under a bike. He came flying down a little hill, entered the yard, turned into the walk, expecting to glide gracefully up to the porch where the girls sat watching.

When the bicycle hit the sand it skidded and turned over. He and the bike plowed up the sand as they came in for a landing at the feet of the astonished girls!

He jumped up, leaving the bicycle, and took off without saying a word. The laughter of the girls followed him as he headed for the barn. Can't we all remember instances when, as teen-agers, we tried to impress our peers, just as disastrously?

Little Sister and Her Cousins

"Spending the day" with children along can present problems. Little Sister always had problems when two little cousins came to see her. Their parents visited only in the summer, and after dinner, the adults sat on the front porch, and Little Sister was told to take her cousins, a boy and a girl, into the house to play with her toys. They were both a little younger than she, but her toys were very dear to her, and she objected loudly when anyone mistreated them. The cousins followed a pattern—they always wanted the same toy, and it was a tug-of-war to see which one would be the victor. The toy was usually the loser. Most of the time Little Sister sat helplessly, just hoping the toy would survive.

This particular afternoon as the cousins looked over the toys Little Sister spotted her latest acquisition: a doll, that was so dear to her she could not bear to have them touch it. She attempted to slip the doll away, before they saw it, but she was too late. This time it was a three-way tug-of-war. She soon saw the doll would be pulled apart, as no one would turn loose. This called for drastic action! What could she do? She had little time to think about it, so she did the only thing she could think of—she bit them! She bit each one on the arm. Of course, bedlam broke loose!

"She bit me! She bit me!" They went screaming to their mother. Little Sister, holding her doll tightly, followed them. She could not deny what she had done, for the print of her teeth was plainly visible on their arms. In her defense she did say that she did not want them to play with her new doll for fear they would break it.

Her mother took the doll, and told Little Sister she must apologize for what she had done. Grudgingly she obeyed. The children were told to go back to play and this time to behave themselves. To her surprise, Little Sister had no further problems with those cousins!

Why Can't I Have Some?

This story occurred in the Christian Church, and illustrates how unhappy children can be when they do not understand certain rituals that take place in our churches.

The pastor continued to preach, and as the noon hour approached, one could see the little boy's eyes turning often, with increasing longing, toward the sacramental table covered with its linen cloth, and with dishes shining through the transparent net.

Hunger was written all over the face of the youngster, who was attending this service with his beloved Uncle John. As his uncle took his place in serving the Holy Sacrament, the child's face lighted up, at last it was time to eat! But then the trays were passed over his outstretched hand, tears of disappointment rolled down his face, and he rushed out of the church.

The uncle left the church as quickly as he could, but his nephew was nowhere in sight. He rushed to his home, which was only a short distance from the church, and there he found the little boy. He was in his aunt's arms sobbing, and saying over and over, "I'm never going to church again with Uncle John. He served refreshments to everyone except me, and I was so hungry."

I Believe the Bible from Lid to Lid

A retired minister was asked to preach at the Methodist church one Sunday. He was a tall, stately gentleman, well known in the Auburn area, but he had a tendency, when preaching, to become excited.

At one point in the sermon, he held the Bible high over his head, and shouted, "Some people don't believe the Bible, but I believe it from lid to lid. Some people don't believe that Jonah swallowed the whale, but I do!"

He never knew he had made a mistake, but that day the congregation had a difficult time trying to keep from laughing!

My Little Black Woman

On another occasion this same minister was teaching a Sunday Schol class at the Methodist Church, and was trying to make a point of how important a minister's wife could be to the success of her husband. He spoke fondly of his wife as, "My little black-eyed woman," but this day he repeatedly called her, "My little black woman"!

There Was No Doubt Who Made the Bread

The father and mother had gone to the 11 o'clock service of the revival meeting. As it was a weekday, the three teen-aged sons had been left at home to do some chores and to cook dinner for the family.

The boys decided to show off their culinary skills, and drew straws to see who would cook what! The one designated to make corn bread to go with the fresh beans and potatoes wanted to make some real fancy bread. He decided it must go in the long bread pan. He couldn't remember when he had seen that much corn bread before. He smoothed it down with a spoon, then patted it with his hand. Wouldn't it look good with his name on it? Wouldn't his parents be surprised to come home and see "autographed corn bread" on the table? He took his finger and making deep imprints, wrote TOM, in large letters down the length of the dough in the pan. He was immensely pleased with himself, and the skill he had demonstrated in autographing that bread. He looked at it several times as it cooked to be sure his name still stood out clearly. It did, deep and clear.

The boys knew about what time their parents would return from church, so they set the table, put the food in serving dishes, and were putting the dishes on the table when they heard voices. They had finished just in time. They lined up in the dining room to receive their parents' praise for a job well done. The autographed bread had been placed in the middle of the table, and turned so that they could read TOM without any trouble.

When the parents entered, they were not alone, the minister was with them, and all eyes fell on the autographed bread. Needless to say, the maker of the bread was not as jubilant as he had been a few minutes earlier. He didn't know what his parents would do to him after the minister left. He felt disgraced—he wouldn't have had the minister see what he had done for anything! His brothers thought it was a great joke and enjoyed every minute of his embarrassment.

It didn't turn out so badly after all. His parents scolded him, but he didn't get the whipping he feared.

The Power of a Sneeze

Everything was as quiet as a pin dropping as the congregation sat spell-bound listening to the visiting minister. Emotions were soaring to a high pitch, when suddenly a roof-raising sneeze pierced the stillness, and the preacher's dentures went flying through the air, landing with a neat "plunk" at the feet of the lady on the front seat. Very graciously, she picked up the dentures and returned them to their owner, as he began the shortest benediction the congregation ever heard!

Just Ask My Wife

The minister had called an unexpected business meeting one evening at the end of the service. One church official who was tired and sleepy, sat with his head against the wall sound asleep. The exasperated chairman of the meeting called upon the sleeping man for his opinion. There was no answer—again came the question. The wife was frantically shaking her husband. By the time the question came for the third time, the sleeping man was aroused, "What's that? What do I think?" Then with a laugh he said, "Just ask my wife! She does the talking for the family." This bit of humor smoothed away everyone's weariness, and the meeting continued.

Ministers Aren't Always Polite

It was always a big occasion when the minister came to dinner, but the food sometimes ran short. This particular Sunday there were more guests for dinner than had been expected, and the two boys in the family had to wait, much to their disgust.

They stood behind the half-open kitchen door, and hungrily watched as the food was being passed. Everyone seemed to be having a wonderful time except the boys. The fried chicken was being passed the second time, and when it reached the minister he took the last two pieces, and commented: "This chicken is delicious!"

The boys had watched him take the last of the chicken, and one of them spoke out in a clearly audible voice, "Old hog, take it all!"

Sitting Up With the Dead

Years ago, in small towns, when there was a death in the community, it was customary for the body to be returned to the home, and remain there until time for the funeral. People in the community came to sit up with the body at night to show their respect, and allow the family to sleep. Food was sent in by the neighbors and those who "sat up" had a feast. It was really a social occascion. Young people liked to come because it gave them a chance to be together, and there was always a lot of good food. But sometimes unusual things happened.

The death of this staunch church member had been expected, and a large number of people had been coming and going all evening. Now the family had retired, and it was well after midnight. As the weather was warm, the doors and the windows were open, and no one in town thought of locking a door, even if it was past midnight.

Two of the ladies decided to go to the kitchen to make coffee. When the coffee was ready they invited everyone to come into the dining room, and partake of the food that had been sent in. It was almost like a party, everyone talking and thoroughly enjoying the food. They were having such a good time, they lingered for quite awhile.

When they returned to the room where the body lay, the women began screaming, and everyone ran from the house!

While they were in the dining room, some mischievous boys had entered the room through the unlocked door, propped the body up in the coffin, put a flower (from a nearby vase) in his mouth, and a flower in each hand! It proved to an un-nerving experience.

His First Funeral

The minister at the Methodist Church in Auburn was a young ministerial student from Emory University, who had never conducted a funeral before, and was fearful of making a mistake.

Finally, the inevitable happened, and he had to conduct his first funeral service. He had many misgivings, afraid that he might bungle the whole thing.

The pianist was playing the piano, and a quartet was singing. All at once, the casket began to move toward the piano and the unsuspecting pianist. The young minister could not believe his eyes. In fact, he thought he must be so scared he was "seeing things." He wondered if he were about to faint, and would fall on the floor. But, no, that casket WAS moving, because it was nearer the piano. He jumped to his feet and shouted, "Look Out"!

The quartet looked around, and the one nearest the casket stepped forward, and stopped it—the quartet continued to sing! Although it was the dead of winter, the minister mopped the perspiration from his brow.

By this time, one of the undertakers had come forward to relock the casket wheels that had somehow come unlocked. The minister finished the service without further mishap, but this was one funeral he would never forget.

Whose Funeral Did I Preach?

Mr. K. was an outstanding figure in his rural community, a leader, and active worker in his church. Now he was lying at death's door. His circuit-rider pastor, living some distance away, visited him as often as circumstances permitted, and although knowing the seriousness of his condition, was shocked when a message was relayed to him requesting that he conduct Mr. K's funeral.

Because of the distance involved, he was unable to go to Mr. K's home before the funeral, but went directly to the church. The service was beginning as he reached the church, so he went straight to the pulpit. He gave a touching eulogy of Mr. K, elaborating upon the great loss to the community and to the church at the passing of this good man. So enthralled was he at the great loss facing everyone, he did not notice the looks of amazement and consternation on the faces of those listening to his praise of the man lying in the casket.

At the close of the sermon the casket was opened, as is still the custom in some rural churches, and friends and relatives walked by to take a last look at the deceased. As the minister looked down upon the upturned face, he gave a gasp of horror! His face became as white as the one he gazed upon. He clutched the casket for support.

At last the service was over, and as the minister turned from the grave, he grasped a friend's arm saying, "Who in Heaven's name is that man we've just buried?" The friend looked at the minister strangely, "You really didn't know *who* he was? That explains the sermon you preached. He was the nee'r-do-well brother of Mr. K. He left home years ago, a real tough guy, always in trouble. He was killed, and his body was shipped back for burial. Thank goodness, Mr. K. was too sick to know what was going on here!"

The minister walked away, his head bent low, as if he

carried the burdens of the world upon his shoulders. How could he ever correct this horrible mistake?

There was no way to separate the Church from the social life and customs in the community. The Church was the hub around which the life of the little town of Auburn revolved. People didn't always like or agree with the pastors of the churches, but they went to church, and enjoyed seeing each other and being with friends.

I will close this chapter with one final story, in a lighter vein, but which expresses the way many of us have felt when attending church.

Timid? Not She!

Little Sister was not quite three. Her mother had never taken her to a church service for fear she would get restless and cry.

Her older sister, who was a teen-ager, begged to be allowed to take Little Sister to a big "tent meeting" which would be held in the open. Finally her mother agreed.

They went into the tent and sat with some other teenage girls, who said they would help take care of Little Sister.

It was a long service. The visiting minister preached for about an hour, and then there was a special song service. After that the pastor said he had a few more words to say. Everyone grew restless, especially Little Sister. She would not sit still. Finally, she stood up on the bench, pointed her finger at the minister, and said at the top of her voice, "Man sit down! Man sit down!" There were many inaudible "Amens" said by the congregation. Little Sister was not taken to church again until she could be relied upon not to break up the service.

Chapter 4

COME ON, LET'S GO TO "BIG MEETIN' "

In July and August, when crops were laid-by (plowing and hoeing finished), revivals or protracted meetings would begin. Every church had a revival, and it usually lasted a week. Services began one Sunday and ended the next, with a baptizing in the afternoon. Even in the Methodist churches there were often some who preferred immersion to sprinkling. Revival services gave young and old alike a chance to be together and socialize. This was vacation time for farmers, and business was always slow during

49

these two months, so it was not unusual for stores to be closed during services. Young people looked forward to two months of dressing-up and going out twice each day and being with others. Choirs of young people were formed for services, and many times the same group went from church to church following the revivals. It was a time of fun, dating, and a general good time.

Meetings were usually emotional, typically the "hell fire and brimstone" kind of preaching, and shouting. People might be clapping hands, singing and crying while walking up and down the aisles of the church, "shouting." Shouting could lead to hilarious episodes, and unexpected results.

First Her Hair Went Down—Then her Skirt

The first time I ever saw a person shout was at the Auburn Baptist Church. She was a tall stately lady, who always wore shirtwaists and long dark skirts with wide belts, and hair drawn back from her face in a knot at the nape of her neck. She was a Gibson girl type. The congregation was singing when she felt moved to shout. She left her seat, went down the aisle clapping her hands and tossing her head from side to side. As she went down the aisle toward the front of the church, her hair came loose and began sliding gradually down her back. The placket of her skirt came open—this was before the day of zippers—and slipped from under her belt, revealing a white petticoat. The full skirt slipped lower and lower in the back, the front was held firmly by the belt. As she crossed the front of the church, hair down her back, skirt trailing behind her, and white petticoat showing, all eyes were upon her. The congregational singing was the only thing that prevented the giggles from being heard. As she reached the aisle, she realized her skirt was about to fall to the floor, but she kept going, and when she reached the back door, out she went! She did not return to the church that night, and no one else shouted during the service. I remember nothing else about what took place that night, but the mental picture of how that lady looked is still clear and vivid to me today.

She Is Coming After Us!

My sister related her own first experience with shouting. This occurred before I was born. Sister, along with several young cousins, were visiting my father's brother and his wife. This aunt was a very religious person, a devout Baptist, and she was taking the young people to revival services that evening. At the supper table she talked to them about joining the church, and said she sincerely hoped some of them would be moved to answer the minister's call that night and unite with the church.

The cousins ranged in age from nine to twelve, and they were uneasy about attending the service. Although Auntie was sitting down front with the adults, they planned to sit near the back of the church.

The minister pleaded with the "unsaved" to join the church before it was too late. Emotions rose to a high pitch and the young cousins saw their aunt rise. She was clapping her hands and singing loudly. As she started toward the rear of the church, one of the cousins whispered, "She's coming after us—let's hide!" They all dived under the bench and huddled quietly on the floor until she returned to her seat. Those sitting around the girls were amused and looked at each other knowingly, and understood their reason for hiding. The girls were glad they were being picked up by another relative after service, because they did not want to face their aunt again that night.

A Shower of Cookies

This same aunt always made teacakes to take to revival meeting, because she felt sorry for the small children who got so tired and restless during the long services. When a child became restless and cried, she would pass some of her teacakes to the child, and this seemed to work like magic. This particular night she had passed out teacakes several times and had forgotten to close the large bag she carried them in. I believe these bags were called reticules. Anyway, a few minutes later, she felt the call to shout. She stood up, began waving her arms, and then started clapping her hands—and cookies started flying everywhere. Instead of "showers of blessings," they had showers of cookies, and she was unaware of what was happening. Children began to dive around under benches trying to retrieve the tea-cakes.

Coming to the Aid of the Minister

My brother-in-law, the late Tom G. Ethridge, had his favorite story that introduced him to the phenomenon, we call Shouting.

The minister was having little success getting people to come to the "mourner's bench" for prayer, nor would they respond to his invitation to join the church. He made one proposition after another trying to get some response from the congregation. A lady parishoner, feeling sorry for the pastor, and considering it her duty to come to his aid, turned to the lady sitting beside her and said, "If you will hold my baby for me, I'll make Old Glory hump-it"!. (Hump-it means to move, to hurry.)

She rose to her feet, clapping her hands and shouting, "Praise the Lord," over and over. She was quite successful, and "revived" the meeting in a big way!

Hanging From a Nail

My mother could remember the days of hoop skirts. As a child she witnessed a scene she never forgot. To be in fashion one would be obliged to wear a hoop skirt, even when it was not practical; and in hot weather an excessive number of petticoats could be uncomfortable. It was a temptation to leave off any under garments that were not absolutely necessary. This particular fashionably dressed hoop-skirted lady, became quite emotional during a revival service, and began shouting. She jumped up on the bench, clapping her hands and began to sing. All went well until she tried to step down. Her skirt caught on a nail in the back of the bench, and turned her upside down, where she hung helplessly. What a sight—it brought that meeting to a hasty close!

A Study in Geography

Often during evening revival meetings in late summer the church could not accommodate all those who came. People came from far and near, simply to have somewhere to go. The churches were hot and uncomfortable, and there were always some men and boys who had no intention of going inside the church. They stood outside around wagons, buggies, and cars talking and enjoying themselves. As they swapped stories, arguments sometimes developed, and these arguments could lead to fights. If a loud argument or fight occurred the group would move far enough from the church so that the worshipers would not be disturbed.

On one hot summer night, at a country church a mile or so from Auburn, two men had an argument that resulted in a fight. the man who was losing, pulled a knife and stabbed his opponent. Onlookers rushed the injured man into Auburn to a doctor. Those in the church knew nothing about the incident until services were over.

One of the witnesses to the fight was eagerly trying to inform those who came out of the church about the dreadful fight that had taken place. People crowded around him to hear the details. As he repeated the story he embellished it until he scarcely recognized it himself! Finally, someone managed to get in a question. "Just where was he stabbed?" It suddenly dawned on the "newsy witness" that he did not know the answer to that question—but he could never admit it. So he excitedly replied, "Why, he was cut from Dan to Beersheba!" Now, if you remember your Biblical map—that is quite a distance. In fact, it would have been about the distance from Murphy, N.C. to Newnan, Ga. How many understood the implications of his reply is an unanswered question, but it stopped further questions from being asked!

The Price a Minister Must Pay

A young ministerial student from Emory became pastor of the Methodist Church in Auburn. He was conducting his first revival meeting, and was trying to appear experienced and sure of himself.

The weather was hot, and the windows were opened wide to let in as much air as possible. The church was packed with people, as it was the first service of the revival. The Sunday night service was always better attended than the other night services. There was an unusual number of bugs flying around the lights, and the light over the pulpit was quite bright. The young minister was preaching a very forceful sermon, and the congregation was attentive. He opened his mouth to make a statement, and in flew a big moth! Everyone gasped. What would he do? The look of surprise on his face faded away. With a determined effort he swallowed, and the moth went down. The congregation heaved a sigh of relief, and the minister continued his sermon.

Take Aim and Fire

We were attending a young people's meeting at the Auburn Baptist Church. The unusual feature of this evening's program was the fact that one of the town's "bad-boys," who had recently joined the church during the revival, was leading the devotional. Looking over the congregation, we recognized two boys who in the past had shared many reckless escapades with him. We wondered if they might try to cause trouble.

The young man read the Scripture and gave his talk, amidst constant restless fidgeting, whispering, mocking smirks, and subdued laughter from his former pals. Throughout his talk the speaker kept a watchful eye on the boys, as though speculating on their next move. His speech finished, he knelt in prayer by the front pew and as he prayed, his face an open target, his former pals hit him in the center of his forehead with a spitball. After rubbing his forehead, the kneeling boy reached for the spitball lying on the seat by him, with one eye open, he took deadly aim and sent it flying full blast at the leader of his tormentors, who was convulsed in subdued laughter. The spitball hit his nose with a dull thud. Shocked incredulity and chagrin covered the victim's countenance, as he and the kneeling boy eyed each other unflinchingly. Slowly the two tormentors sat back in their seats shamefacedly, as the boy ended his prayer with thanksgiving for being able to cling to the right. (Yes, our eyes were open during the prayer, and we saw it all.)

The Water Was Not For Him

After revivals came baptizings. They were held at a lake or pond. Park's Mill Pond, a short distance from Auburn, was the nearest place for the Auburn churches to hold baptizings. They were usually held on Sunday afternoon, after the meeting had closed on Friday or Saturday night.

It was Sunday afternoon and the Auburn Baptist Church was holding its baptizing at Park's Mill. One boy, who must have been ten or twelve years old, was dressed out in a new outfit for the occasion—green knee pants and a white shirt but with bare feet. He obviously was having misgivings about going into the water.

He was next in line, when suddenly he decided it was not for him, and up a tree he went! His parents pleaded, then threatened, still he would not budge. Finally, his older sister, who had a stubborn streak herself, told him if he didn't come down he would be sorry. These words conveyed some hidden message he evidently understood, and he came down without a word. Large crowds came to baptizings, and everyone was watching to see what would happen next.

He went into the water silently, with a determined and unhappy look on his face. He came up out of the water as if shot from a gun, noisily blowing water from his nose and mouth. He did not stop as he bounded out of the

water, with green dye, from his green pants, running down his bare legs and feet. He left the water running, and was still running when he disappeared from sight.

He later told some of his boy friends that it took him a week to get all that green dye off his body, and he vowed he was never going to church again!

Unexpected Advertising

People often used feed and fertilizer sacks to make clothes. Feed sacks were made of pretty prints, and fertilizer sacks were an off-white in color, but when washed were soft and durable. The only difficulty was the printing that appeared on the fertilizer bags — it was hard to bleach out the large letters. If at first the lettering did not bleach out satisfactorily, frequent washings would do the trick. Men's work shirts and underwear, and sometimes ladies' underwear were made from fertilizer sacks.

Women often liked to wear white when being baptized.

On this particular Sunday one lady, who was decidedly
hefty, was giving the two ministers some difficulty in low-
ering her into the water. But that was not the cause of the
giggling among the crowd, as she finally came up out of
the water. Her thin white dress was clinging to her body,
and clearly discernible through her dress and across her
rear, were the words, "Green's Favoritie'" a common
brand of fertilizer. When dry, the words did not show up,
and the material had been slightly gathered, and had made
a nice shadow-proof slip. When wet and plastered against
her body, the words were quite plainly visible.

Chapter 5

FROM COLLEGE TO THE 'TATER PATCH
PERRY-RAINEY COLLEGE

Auburn was an educational center from 1893 to 1924. The Mulberry Baptist Association, composed of Gwinnett, Jackson, and Hall Counties, established a secondary boarding school there in 1893, and it was called Mulberry High School. The school was such a success that it was expanded and became a college in 1894, and given the name Perry-Rainey College. Hiram T. Rainey, an outstanding Baptist minister, and William T. Perry, a successful farmer and business man, were instrumental in organizing the college, so the school was named for them.

Many homes in the Auburn and Carl communities became "boarding houses" to accommodate the students who came from many sections of the state. Dormitories were built for both boys and girls, but it required some time to complete them. J.A. Bagwell was principal of Mulberry High School, and remained as President of the College until 1897. He was a native of Auburn and had graduated from Mercer in 1892.

The first graduation took place in May 1896. The 11 graduates were: George Bagwell, Bertha Blakey, Justus Blakey, Blanch Cosby, J.C. Flanigan, Truman M. Holland, Bertie Jackson, Maud Jackson, Pearl Jackson, Minnie Perry, and R. Frank Smith.

The *Auburn Messenger*, dated July 26, 1901, carried the announcement of Perry-Rainey College's fall opening, September 16. Their aim in instruction was said to be "Excellence in moral training and thoroughness of mental discipline." The course of study was given as follows:

Freshman: English, American Literature, History, Algebra, and Beginner's Latin.

Sophomore: Rhetoric, Theme Writing, American Literature, History of England, Algebra, Caesar, Beginning Greek.

Junior: Rhetoric, English Literature, Cicero, Xenophon's Anabasis, History of Greece and Rome, and Physics.

Senior: Select English Authors, French, Geology, Trigonometry, Virgil's Aeneid, Herodotus, U.S. History, History of Education, Political Economy, and Pedagogy.

Room and board could be had for $7.00 or $8.00 per
month, and even cheaper by special arrangement. Tuition
was $2.00 per month. Incidentals 5 or ten cents per month.
These figures seem unbelievable when compared to college
costs today.

A new modern brick administration building was built,
at a cost of $15,000 in 1909. By 1907, the Georgia Baptist
Association owned the school, and it became a prep school
rather than a college. It was known as Perry-Rainey Institute. Its graduates, however, could enter the best colleges
and universities as sophomores, so the quality of scholastic
training remained excellent. A 1907 bulletin of the school
listed four years of Latin and Greek as being requirements.
After it became an Institute, French could be substituted
for Greek.

Perry-Rainey Institute

Although the quality of education in Auburn could be
rated as excellent, the social life patterns of the community
had a lot of "catching-up" to do.

Stepping Out into Society

For weeks everyone had talked of nothing but the
reception to be given by the faculty for all the high school
students. This was their first official step into society.
None of the students had ever been to a reception. Many
members of the faculty were just out of college and hoped
to make this as spectacular as those they'd known in
school. It was to be held in the lovely new administration
building. All of this took precedence over other school
activities, even among the teachers. Every girl had to have
a new dress, and every mother tried to make her daughter's
dress prettier than any other. There would be no evening
dresses, just a nice Sunday dress. Some of the bigger boys
had long pants, but the majority of boys still wore short

pants (called knee pants), as clothes were worn as long as
they were usable.

Word leaked out that the ladies of the faculty were
going to wear real evening dresses! The excitement grew.
Word came that the refreshments would be punch, cake,
and jello, and the students were filled with awe. What WAS
punch? Did you eat it or drink it? And jello, what did it
look like? The boys went around hitting one another
saying, "I'll punch you," laughing loudly, not realizing
how silly they were.

At last the big night came. Each home was lighted as
brightly as possible with kerosene lamps, so that proud
parents could admire the beautiful clothes modeled by
their daughters. They looked to see if their sons wore
ties, and had shined their heavy shoes.

As the students went down the receiving line, most of
them were able to say, "Hello," and shake hands, but some
were too shy to do either. The students had all heard from
various churches about the "sins of the world," well, here it
was, right before their eyes—the lady teachers in their
evening dresses, with no sleeves and such scandalous necks!
But there wasn't a girl present who would not have gladly
traded for a dress without a yoke and collar. The boys
were just "bug eyed," and fascinated beyond words.
Even the prettiest girls realized that the lady teachers had
stolen the show.

Then they spied the punch table. Again the boys were
giving each other punches, and covering their embarrassment with hilarious laughter. They tasted the punch with
what they hoped was sophistication, and found it delicious. Some of the more brazen went back for seconds,
and all wished they might. The girls' high buttoned shoes
began to hurt, and they envied the boys who were wearing
their shined old school shoes.

After much walking around and standing against the

wall trying to get another look at those "sinful" evening
dresses, the students were ushered into the dining hall
where small center tables, covered with white cloths, had
been set up. These were the same kind of little tables that
graced the center of front rooms and parlors in the community. A little bowl of red flowers in the center of each
table brought out the redness of the jello placed in des-
sert dishes before each guest. The small tables made conversation rather intimate for each two couples seated
there. At one table, the four young people hesitatingly
took their first taste of jello, and one of the boys remarked,
"Look at this stuff shake—it's as scared as we are!"

Not one of those boys and girls would ever forget the
thrill and exictement found in that "most wonderful social
event of their lives."

Outstanding ministers, educators, lecturers, and poli-
ticians came to Perry-Rainey to speak. Commencement
exercises were occasions of great importance. Crowds of
people came to Auburn, as families and friends of the
students wanted to be present for the greatest event of the
year. Almost every house in Auburn and Carl had visitors
for the occasion.

The commencement sermon was delivered by a famous
minister; the literary address given by an equally important
speaker. The plays, declamations, and music recitals were
looked forward to, but the debate between the Literary
Societies was the highlight of commencement. Two
speakers from each society (Claric-Sophic and Alpha-
Sigma) were chosen for the debate. To be chosen as a de-
bator was the greatest honor to be won in the college. It
was said that the quality of these debates could compare
favorably with any school in the state.

The school offered other forms of entertainment to
the community. Plays, recitals, and lectures were outstanding events. The yearly visits of Chautauqua were a great

educational treat for the community. Some of America's best known lecturers, pianists, and singers toured with Chautauqua.

She Had Presence of Mind

At graduation the girls dressed in white, and when their names were called to receive their deplomas, large baskets of flowers were brought down the aisle to the stage and presented to them. It was almost a popularity contest to see which girl would receive the most flowers. If a girl received several baskets of flowers, two or three girls would walk down the aisle together to deliver them.

To deliver flowers was a special honor, and the pastel colored dresses the flower girls wore were always beautiful. One evening, these flower girls were lined up at the rear of the auditorium with their baskets on the floor behind them, waiting for the first diploma to be delivered. Their dresses came to their ankles, and their full skirts gave evidence of ruffled petticoats underneath. The first girl-graduate's name was called. Three girls promptly picked up their baskets and walked down toward the stage. The girl in the middle seemed to be having trouble. All at once, her petticoat fell around her feet but she did not falter. She stepped carefully out of it, and kicked it to one side, continued to the stage, delivered the basket, then turned and walked to the rear of the auditorium as if nothing had happened!

What happened to the petticoat? A girl sitting on the front row, stepped forward, picked it up, and tiptoed out the side entrance to return it to its owner.

Courting in the Cold

My sister had a cousin visiting her. Pearl had come from Jefferson to attend some special event being held at Perry-Rainey. As this was a weekend, she had a chance to meet many of the young people in town when they attended church on Sunday. One of the boys, who was not popular with the girls, asked her for a date Sunday night. She told him she already had a date. He then wanted to know if he could come to see her Monday night. She did not want a date with him, so she said she might go home Monday, although she knew she was not going home until Wednesday.

Monday proved to be a chilly day, and that night found the family gathered around an open fire in the master bedroom.

The doorbell rang. At the door stood William; he asked if Pearl had gone home. I had answered the door and was

always ready to volunteer information. I told him she was
still with us, in fact, she was not going home until Wednesday. He was invited into the parlor, and Pearl was called.
She came in reluctantly. There was no fire in the parlor,
and she made no effort to build one. They talked for
nearly an hour, when he announced he was going home, as
he was about to freeze.

She came back to the bedroom laughing, and said that
at last she had learned how to get rid of him. He did not
even mention trying to see her again.

On Tuesday night the family was busy clearing the
table and getting ready to wash dishes, when the doorbell
rang. As everyone was busy Pearl said she would go to the
door. She opened the door, and there stood William,
carrying a big armload of wood and kindling. He walked
in unceremoniously and started to build a fire in the parlor
fireplace, stating that he did not intend to freeze *that*
night!

We Are Going to Pray

A young man from Lawrenceville who was attending
school at Perry-Rainey, was noted for his glib tongue. He
was quite a "lady's man," and was enamored of the pretty
music teacher at the school. He always tried to sit next to
her in the dining hall. It was the custom when everyone
was seated, for the Dean or some other designated official,
to call on someone to return thanks. That particular night,
after everyone else had gotten quiet for the blessing to be
said, the young man continued to whisper to the music
teacher. The Dean had been gazing at him steadily; suddenly
he called on the young man to return thanks. Not being
in the habit of offering any kind of prayer, his usually
glib tongue was silent. Realizing he must say something,
but totally unable to think of anything appropriate, he
said, "Look out Lord, we're gonna eat!"

Southeastern Christian College

During 1914-15, the Georgia Baptist Association nego-
tiated with the Christian Denomination to buy Perry-
Rainey. The Baptist Church simply could not afford to
support the large number of schools it had been operating.
Southeastern Christian College officially opened in the fall
of 1915.

A new group of faculty member came to Auburn.
They were mostly married men with families. This in-
creased the town's supply of children and created a demand for houses.

Two of the faculty members at Southeastern Christian
College, I remember quite well. One was a Mr. Parish, who
willingly played his violin at different community gather-
ings. He could play classical music, but I loved to hear him
play, "Arkansas Traveler," and other country music. He
also sang as he played. The other teacher was John V.
Thomas, a minister and English professor. He was tall and
dark, with a black mustache, and a grin like President
Jimmy Carter's. He was my idea of the perfect villain! He
only needed a dagger between his teeth! He remained in
Auburn after the college closed, and farmed, as well as
raising chickens. He had no experience in farming—everything was done by "the book," but he was quite successful, which goes to show that one can read and study, and
become a good farmer without previous experience. His
success certainly surprised people in the community.

A Prayer of Thanksgiving

The unmarried members of the faculty at the new college had been invited out to dinner in one of the private
homes in the community. As they went in to dinner, the
host asked Professor Williams if he would return thanks.
The teacher said he would be glad to ask the blessing. They
sat down around the large lazy-susan table, had the bless-

ing, and enjoyed a delicious home cooked meal. Everyone
had finished, and comments were made as to how good the
food had been. Professor Williams had raised his water
glass to take a drink, when his host asked him to offer a
prayer of thanksgiving for the food they had enjoyed.
Professor Williams was so surprised and startled, that he
choked! He had already given thanks once, what was he
supposed to say the second time? When he finally stopped
coughing, he still didn't utter a sound. The lady teacher,
(who happened to be my sister) sitting next to him, tapped
him on the knee and whipsered, "Say something." He
regained his composure, and gave a proper prayer of
thanksgiving!

'Tater Patch School

Southeastern Christian College created one problem
for the community. Perry-Rainey had allowed the local
elementary school to be housed in one of the buildings on
the campus, and the Christian College was willing to in-
clude high school grades in its curriculum, but not elementary grades. The community was faced with the
problem of finding land and erecting a public school building by the time school opened in the fall of 1915. The
college gave them permission to tear down an old building
on the campus and use the lumber in the construction of
the public school. The site chosen for the new building
was where Roy Park's home now stands on Myrtle Street.

Mr. Charlie Duncan had planted sweet potatoes on the
land chosen for the new school. P.R. Chesser, who seemed
to be in charge of the construction, said the school must
be finished by September. Mr. Duncan wanted to harvest
his potatoes before construction began. As a result of this
heated controversy the school became known as the
" 'Tater Patch," and was never called by any other name.

This school was used by the community until after

Southeastern Christian College closed in 1924. A bond
issue was floated in 1928 to buy the property from the
Christian Church. The old administration building was
then purchased and became known as Auburn Consoli-
dated School. It was used by the community until it was
pronounced unsafe for occupancy. The building was torn
down and replaced by the present modern building and
gymnasium.

The land on which the present school stands can only
be used for educational purposes. If not so used it goes
back to the heirs of J.O. Hawthorne, and J.J. Wages, who
originally gave the land. The Auburn school has the dis-
tinction of being the only school property in the county
owned by the people of the community.

I started to school at the 'Tater Patch, and I remember
my first sweetheart. He was red-headed and freckled faced;
his last name was Beddingfield, but I don't remember his
first name. I was in the second grade when I entered, since
I could already read and write, but the first two grades
played together. Jump-the-rope was a favorite game, but
the thing we liked most was running up a board that had
been placed against the high end of the front porch. This
was hard to do since it was quite steep. "Young Mr. Beddingfield" would stand on the porch and give me his hand
when I started up the board! Ah, the things we remember!

We lined up in the hall one grade behind the other for
a brief devotional each morning. The principal, the Rev.
J.B. Brookshire, read the Bible, and led us in several religious songs before we went to our rooms. Two of his favorite songs were: Onward Christian Soldiers, and Let
Jesus Come Into Your Heart. He was short, but very
lively, and he wore nose glasses. When leading the singing,
he took off his glasses and waved them around in the air
like a baton.

I See Him, I See Him!

My husband had Mr. Brookshire for an English teacher and they were studying Washington Irving's *Legend of Sleepy Hollow*. Mr. Brookshire was reading the description of Ichabod Crane as he fled from the headless horseman, with his coat-tails flapping behind him in the wind. Mr. Brookshire had become quite enthralled in the story. He paused, removed his nose glasses, and said, "Class, can't you just see him riding down that road?" The class dutifully agreed, except for Alvin, my husband's cousin. He shook his head and solumnly said, "No Sir, I can't see him." Mr. Brookshire put on his glasses and scowled at Alvin, "All right, I'll read it again and you listen carefully." The students were beginning to giggle, but Alvin sat with a solemn face. Just as Mr. Brookshire was completing the passage a second time, Alvin spoke up excitedly, "I see him, I see him!" Mr. Brookshire beamed with satisfaction.

Thinking back over this period when Auburn was noted for its excellent educational opportunities, I realize it really marks the end of an era. Churches could no longer finance so many denominational schools, and they had outlived their usefulness, since State colleges were replacing them. But the closing of such schools spelled ruin for many small towns. They could not finance good schools themselves, so people "for their children's sake" moved away to larger towns, where the schools were better.

Chapter 6

CHRISTMAS, COUNTRY STYLE

Christmas was a wonderful time for children and grownups alike. The week before Christmas was baking week at our house. My mother always baked five or six cakes, storing them in round hat boxes surrounded by apples, which kept them moist. The dining room table and sideboard were filled with plates of Christmas candies. My favorite was coconut candy, made from fresh grated coconut colored pink and green. The divinity contained black walnut meats, which we picked out. The fudge had hickory nut meats, from our trees in the back yard. Why all this cooking? We must have plenty of food for guests who might drop in, and for the Serenaders and Fantastic Riders, who would be coming during Christmas week.

We decorated our house with garlands of holly hung over the front door, placed on the mantels, and tucked behind pictures. Red paper chains were draped across the two archways, with two red bells hanging from the center loop. The Christmas tree was set up in the parlor just before Christmas. It was decorated with red and green tinsel, tiny red bells, popcorn, small ornaments, and candles in metal holders. One had to be very careful of fire when the candles were lighted. We were one of the few families in town that had a Christmas tree. Family trees were not common in our little community.

I do not remember "Christmas Caroling" being a part of the Christmas festivities. Every house seemed to have some kind of musical instrument, and group singings were so common, both in homes and churches, that there was no thought of going from house to house caroling.

Serenading was like "trick or treating" at Halloween. Serenaders wore costumes and masks, and could be expected any night during Christmas week. Several groups might come by the same evening. They were not children, but young people and adults. Not until years later did children go serenading.

Fantastic Riders came in the day time. They, too, wore costumes and masks. They might come on horse-back or in a two-horse wagon filled with hay. A few came in cars, but at that time cars were still scarce. They were often complete strangers, who came from other communities. Both fastastics and serenaders asked for food. They were eager to perform for cake, candy, or fruit. Buck-dancing and singing were their usual forms of entertainment.

I can never remember a Christmas without a community

Christmas tree. I don't know how far back this custom went, but the *Auburn Messenger* dated December 17, 1902, carried this news item, "The Methodist Church will have a community Christmas Tree and program, on Christmas Eve night." The community tree alternated between the Methodist and Baptist churches for many years, but later it was held only at the Methodist church.

Our Christmas gifts were simple and inexpensive. Many children received only fruit, candy, and raisins for Christmas. To get a small store-bought gift was a wonderful experience. Gifts within the family were usually handmade, as were those exchanged between friends. A girl might get a box of candy, a bought pincushion, a small powder or jewelry box from a boy friend. He might receive a handmade handkerchief, a tie, or perhaps a knitted scarf from her. People had so little that anything was appreciated.

We lived directly behind the Methodist church, and I could watch the big full-grown Christmas tree being hauled in by two horses with the top of the tree extending several feet from the back of the wagon. The tree was usually holly or sweet-smelling cedar. Men and boys set up the tree early Christmas Eve morning, as the young people who would decorate it, arrived about ten o'clock. A fire in the stove would have the church warm by the time the decorators came. To decorate such a large tree was an all-day job. Metal clips were attached to the tree limbs and wax candles placed in these holders. Red and green tinsel (later, silver and gold metallic tinsel) covered the tree. Strings of popcorn, and ingenious handmade decorations added to the beauty of the tree.

Families brought gifts to be hung on the tree, as family Christmas trees were almost unheard of. Sunday School classes drew names, with about 25 cents as the limit for a bought gift, or you could make one if you wished. Friends

exchanged gifts by means of the Christmas tree. If a boy expected to rate with his girl-friend he must have a gift for her on that tree. Packages were usually small, and were really part of the decorations since they hung on the tree. The Sunday School provided small paper bags filled with candy and fruit for every child enrolled in classes. These, too, were hung on the tree. It was a beautiful sight to see a full-grown tree, with its top touching the ceiling, ladened with gifts and bright decorations!

At last night came and it was time for the great event. Families came as a group, soon the church was packed, with people standing in the rear of the building. The children presented a program consisting of songs and recitations.

When the program was over, it was time for Mr. and

Mrs. Santa Claus to arrive. Boys, using ladders, lighted the candles on the tree. What a glorious sight! The children didn't know whether to look for Santa Claus, or at that wonderful tree.

Mr. and Mrs. Santa Claus, in full costume, finally arrived. As they made their way toward the tree, they stopped to speak to children. Boys, still using their ladders, cut the gifts from the tree, and kept a watchful eye for fire. As the gifts were cut from the tree, they were handed one by one, to Santa, and he was told the name on the gift. He, in turn, called out the name in a loud voice, the person would raise his hand, and Mr. or Mrs. Santa delivered the gift, often speculating on its contents.

The church always provided extra gifts suitable for children and adults, in case there might be someone present who had not received a gift. It might be nothing but a handkerchief for an adult, and a bag of fruit and candy for a child, but no one left the church without a gift. Really to the children of the community "Christmas" was that Christmas Tree. So as we left the church, each person with a gift of some kind, there was truly a song in our hearts of "Peace on Earth, Good-will toward Man."

There was one man who was a member of the Methodist church who was a regular "Scrooge." He did not believe in Christmas. He would not buy gifts for his family, but for some reason he always came to the Christmas tree. Since he never received a gift from anyone, the church always presented him with a handkerchief, and he left the church with a big grin on his face.

Who Is This Pretty Girl?

One night, during Christmas, our family decided to go serenading. We had a black girl, Lillian Hosch, living with us, who did the cooking and looked after me. She wanted to go with us, but did not wear a mask. We passed the drug store (actually a soda fountain), and a group of boys who were inside spied us and came outside. They tried to find out who we were. We would change our voices and they were having a difficult time discovering our identity. One boy, who was home for the holidays, was quite interested in Lillian—she was a pretty girl. He thought she had her face blacked. (Remember, we had no bright street lights!) He kept talking to her and she would not say a word. She was wearing a hat and she pulled it down over her face as far as possible, so as to keep her face hidden. The boy put his hand under her chin, raised her face, and kissed her on the mouth! She still said nothing, and dropped her head again.

My brother-in-law, not wishing to embarrass Lillian, told the boys who we were, and also introduced Lillian. When the boys heard her name, they knew who she was, for her parents were well known in the community. It was now the young man's turn to be embarrassed! The other boys never let him forget how anxious he was to "kiss every girl he met on the street."

A Little Long Piece of Cake

A group of serenaders came up on the porch of Little Sister's house one night, and began dancing and calling for food. Her older sister knew they were coming, so she rushed to the door to let them in. Little Sister was right there to welcome them, but when one, wearing a large gray mask shaped like a horse's head, bent down and asked, "Will you get me a little long piece of cake that will fit my mouth?"—she took off! She ran to the back hall and crawled under a sofa. No amount of coaxing would bring her out. That was one night the young people were not bothered by her glib and inquisitive tongue.

I love everything about Christmas—the cooking, the decorating, the buying of gifts, the family tree, but I miss that special feeling of warmth and goodwill we experienced, when the whole community came together for that wonderful community Christmas tree.

I, like my mother, do a lot of baking for Christmas. But I bake cookies. I make over a thousand every Christmas, and give them to friends and shut-ins—it gives me the Christmas spirit!

Chapter 7

FAMILY-LIFE PATTERNS

We were night-people, and this fact was hard to explain in a small town, where 9:30 or 10 o'clock was the accepted bedtime. I was never required to go to bed until the family retired—unless I happened to fall asleep. If I did fall asleep it was understood that a lamp would be left

78

burning in the room I shared with my older sister. My
mother indulged this whim of mine without question,
accepting the fact, I suppose, that the lamp was my "se-
curity blanket." Had she known the real reason for the
lamp, she would literally have raised the roof.

The Witch's Head

Lillian, the daughter of the black nurse I had as a baby,
took care of me and did most of the cooking. She loved to
read and we had a lot of books, but she came up with a
collection of paper-backs about ghosts and witches which
she read to me in the afternoons. My mother, and sister,
when she was not in school, worked at my father's store,
which was next door to our house. Lillian and I had the
house to ourselves in the afternoons. I can remember only
one title of the "scary books" she read to me, but that
book, *The Witch's Head*, was my favorite. The witch's
head was carried around in a suitcase, and when the bag
was opened, out came the witch with long flowing black
hair. I did not dare let my mother know how fearful I had
become. I was constantly listening for footsteps and looking over my shoulder when I heard a noise, expecting to
see that witch glaring at me. Somehow I got the idea the
witch's head stayed in one of our twin parlors. The parlors
were separated by folding doors, but unless we were having
a lot of company, they remained two separate rooms. The
door opening into the second parlor was usually left ajar,
and the least bit of air would make it squeak. When I was
alone I tried to avoid going past that squeaking door, because I was sure the witch made it squeak. My mother
never did find out why I was so afraid of the dark, nor did
she learn about the witch's head.

Spring Thrills

Our family life was controlled by the amount of trade

at the store, and that fluctuated according to the four seasons of the year.

The two things I looked forward to in spring were: being able to play outdoors, and taking off winter underwear, which I detested. Once I put on winter underwear I could not take it off until spring. That made no sense to me because we did have warm days during the winter when it was not needed. I was not allowed to take it off because "you will catch cold." All I could do was wish for Easter, when it could be discarded for another year.

Easter meant new thin dresses, even when it might be cold. I wondered why there was no fear of catching cold at Easter even though a winter coat might feel good. There was one thing I could not do at Easter, even if the temperature was 90 degrees — and that was go barefooted. That

was a privilege to be enjoyed on the first day of May —
never before that date. On May first, regardless of the
weather, I could take off my shoes and go barefooted.
I could never understand the logic in that kind of reason-
ing, but it was the "law and gospel" and I abided by it.

In addition to a new Easter outfit, I looked forward to
egg-hunts at Sunday School, and the arrival of the Easter
Bunny. In front of our house, extending from the store for
half a block, was an avenue of elm trees. Underneath the
elms, day lilies had been planted, and they were beautiful
when they bloomed, but at Easter they were only a few
inches tall. My mother had an oblong sewing basket made
of different colored braid, which I used for my Easter
basket. On Saturday afternoon before Easter I gathered day
lily leaves and filled my basket, placed it in the living room
window, and it was there I found my Easter Eggs on Easter
morning. The leaves were always pressed down as if the
Easter Bunny had been sitting in the basket, and the eggs
were warm. The window was raised a few inches, and I
was assured by my mother that she had left it raised the
night before so the Easter Bunny could come in.

Often dogwood, crabapple, and wild azaleas (wild
honeysuckle) were in bloom at Easter. When they were
blooming we walked to "the rocks," a favorite picnic
spot about half mile from town, where there was a crabapple orchard and lots of wild azaleas. Dogwood and
sweetshrub could be found almost anywhere. We came
home, our arms filled with these wild flowers. We had a
pair of large pink vases about 14 inches tall which stayed
on the mantel in the dining room, and these were always
used for wild flowers. The vases were placed on the hearth
in each of the twin parlors, and the sweet fragrance of the
flowers filled the entire house.

After Easter we considered spring had officially come,
and it was time for me to get the barn loft cleaned so I

could get our play house in order. I said OUR play house, because all my friends came there to play. During the winter, fodder, hay, and other feedstuffs were kept in the barn. Sometimes we had two cows, a mule and a horse, or two horses, and it required a great deal of feed. By spring very little was left in the barn, and that could be stored in a stable. My friends and I worked hard getting everything clean and our "furniture" back in place. The furniture consisted of wooden boxes of different sizes. The wooden boxes shoes came in were so long they made excellent beds and sofas. Higher boxes were just right for tables, and nail kegs made first rate stools. Old curtains strung on wires made room dividers, and could be used for bedspreads and table covers. The barn loft was the place my friends and I sought after school and on Saturdays.

The next big event to look forward to was Commencement Week at Perry-Rainey Institute, later Southeastern Christian College. Southeastern Christian College continued the tradition of Commencement Week. It is hard to realize how important Commencement was to the Auburn community. An education was important to these rural people, very few of the older generation had an opportunity to finish high school much less college. When their sons and daughters were to appear in some event they were going to be there to see them perform. Boarding students expected their parents to be present, too. Most of the boarding students had friends or relatives living in Auburn, so during Commencement there were few homes in town without guests. There was nothing that happened in the community during the entire year that could compare to Commencement. People had to have new clothes to wear to the different events, and somehow we, too, in spite of the store, managed to attend every performance. After this special week was over, we considered summer had arrived, as school was out until next September. Wonderful vacation!

Summer

The only thing I did not like about summer was all the company we had. My sister said we might as well hang out a "Hotel" sign in front of our house. We had several aunts who came every summer and stayed a week. Since our cook was needed at home during the summer, we had all the work to do, and I had a lot of chores. I could sweep, dust, dry dishes, pick and string beans, and gather other vegetables. When we had company my mother didn't like for me to invite children to the house because we were too noisy, neither did she like for me to go visiting.

One nosey aunt always came to the kitchen and criticized the way my sister and I washed dishes. It was the same every summer, she should have realized we were not going to change or else we would have the first time she mentioned it.

One cousin who was about my age came a few times, but we could not get along at all. She did not like anything I had or did. We tried to have a party for her, but the other children couldn't get along with her any better than I could. She soon stopped coming, and I never did go to see her.

Two cousins who visited my sister were very nice. The oldest told me stories, and she could read the Uncle Remus stories better than any one I had ever heard.

Three little cousins, nearer my age, came from Lawrenceville to visit. Lawrenceville was 11 miles from Auburn. They came on the 9:15 train in the morning. Sometimes they came for the day but usually stayed for several days. We four children slept on the floor on pallets—I thought that was great fun. The oldest of the cousins, Thornton, liked corn flakes better than anyone I've ever seen. I think he could have eaten them three times a day and still enjoyed them. When they went home they took the 6:15 train in the evening. They traveled alone for we all knew the conductor on the train would look after them, and their parents would meet them at the station in Lawrenceville.

My mother had a brother, Philip (we called him Uncle Phil), who lived in Sanford, Florida. He came to see us once a year, and arrived by train. He had a strange idea that if he did not let us know when he was coming his visit would be no trouble to us. Of course, the opposite was true. Had we known when he was coming, the guest room would be ready, extra food cooked, and we could have enjoyed his visit much more. We never knew he was in

town until we saw him walking up the street carrying his
bag. He left the same way he came. One morning he would
walk out of the guest room with his bag and announce,
"I think I'd better catch the next train and go visit Sister
Nannie for a few days," and we would not see him again
until next summer when he stepped from the train.

Our home was headquarters for visiting ministers. As
long as Perry-Rainey Institute was in existence we hosted
Baptist ministers—my father was a Baptist. Later, when the
school was sold to the Christian Church, we hosted Christian ministers—my mother and sister were members of the
Christian Church. I never saw a minister who wasn't
hungry.

I remember we prepared for the visit of one Baptist
minister, who was preaching at the Revival services at the
local Baptist Church. We were using our best china and
silver, and I was allowed to set the table. There were five
pieces of silver at each place, and I called my mother to
view my handiwork. She praised me, and I simply could
not wait for dinner time. I was sure the minister would be
impressed by the elegant appearance of that table. He was
impressed, but in a negative way. He looked around the
table, took his hand and pushed the extra pieces of silver
toward the middle of the table and said, "All I need is a
knife and fork." I was crushed and angry that all my work
had been unappreciated. I also thought, "I bet he doesn't
know how to use more than a knife and fork."

The visitors who were the most trouble were the unexpected ones, who came to Auburn for the day, either on
business or shopping—and just "happened" to stop by
the house or store at noon. One had to be hospitable and
extend an invitation to dinner, it was considered "good
business." We sometimes did not have enough food prepared and my mother would have to open extra cans of
food to meet the emergency.

Aside from all our company, there was one more thing I did not like about summer—I always had to take a nap. My mother and sister loved to take naps, so I had to take one. Naps were not required during the rest of the year, so why summer? The only answer I could get to that question was: because summer days are so long. That answer did not satisfy me, and I continued to resist to no avail. Not a person I played with had to take naps—and to this day I will not take a nap in the daytime.

The only whipping I ever received was indirectly related to nap-taking. I had begged to go visit a friend instead of taking a nap. I was told I must have a nap first.

Immediately after the nap I asked again to go play with my friend. The answer was still "No." I continued to beg, and finally my mother told me she was tired of hearing me fuss, and I could not go anywhere.

I took a pair of scissors and began scraping the paint off her new sewing machine. She caught me in the act. I was marched outside to the back yard where she broke a small switch from a peach tree, and whipped my bare legs. If you have never felt the sting of a switch—just be grateful. I knew I did not want another whipping.

Fun in Summer

There was fun connected with summer. We had an annual picnic at my father's mineral springs, and invited friends to go along. It was a beautiful spot so cool and refeshing, but it had one drawback—rattlesnakes. It was located in rattlesnake country, or so the family who lived on my father's land claimed. They told unbelievable tales about the size of rattlers seen at the Springs. I don't believe we saw but one snake the many times we went there, but children were warned not to wander beyond the cleared area. The one rattler we saw was lying next a log that someone was going to sit upon—the snake got away safely, probably as frightened as we were.

There were watermelon cuttings and ice cream suppers, but what I enjoyed most was being invited to someone's orchard to eat peaches—that was simply wonderful. My sister had one big party every summer, given in honor of a guest or some friend's guest. This would be a prom party, with Japanese lanterns strung up in the yard and along the side walk—this was before the day of electric lights. I loved these parties, it was fun watching the grown-ups.

Another thing I enjoyed was spend-the-day parties. It didn't matter to me whether there were children to play with, I enjoyed listening to the adults talk. When we went on such visits my mother drove Old Joe. We had two horses, but she was not allowed to drive Nance because she had a tendency to run away and didn't like women. Anyone could drive Joe, provided you could make him go! He poked along at such a slow pace my mother would declare she would never drive him again. She would smile slyly and say the next time she went somewhere she was going to drive Nance. However, Joe always came to life when we started home. He somehow knew he was on his way to his barn and pasture, and it was all my mother could do to keep him from running away, and she lost interest in driving Nance.

The long days of summer were a delight, and I could stay out and play until dark. Then I liked to curl up in one of the two swings on our big front porch and dream about what I was going to be when I grew up. I thought about all the wonderful places we read about in winter, sitting before an open fire. I knew I had to go West and visit the places Zane Grey wrote about in his novels. I loved James Oliver Curwood's tales of the far North Country, but I was not keen on cold weather, so that did not tempt me. Sometimes my sister would go inside and play the piano—I liked that because it gave me music to dream by.

Special Friends

My first playmates were the Maxwell twins, Loyd and Floyd. They lived right behind our store. We had a play-house underneath the back of our house, which was not underpinned at that time. We were not old enough to go to school, but were at the mudpie stage. Their father was cashier of the Auburn bank, and they later moved to Winder.

My next playmate was Lila Pool who lived on the street back of us. I could stand in my backyard and whistle and she would come out, and we would meet at our back fence and talk. Our talk centered around getting together to play. When neither of our parents could be cajoled into letting us visit, we wrote letters and put them in our secret post office near the fence. The song we whistled as a signal was "My Little Girl, at least I think that was the title—anyway the words began: "My little girl, I know I love you, and I think of you each day . . . ."

When the weather was hot, the barn loft was unbearably hot, so I had a playhouse underneath two hickory trees in our backyard. There was a rope swing on one of the limbs. Lila had a playhouse in her side yard under black walnut trees, she also had a swing. My playhouse was shady in the morning, and hers in the afternoon, so we spent many happy hours in them.

Playing paper dolls was another favorite occupation in summer. I brought old magazines and catalogues from home and we spent hours cutting out paper dolls sitting on the floor of their upstairs hall, right in front of the door that opened onto a porch that extended across the front of their house. We were not allowed to play on the porch, but the hall was very cool.

In the evenings we liked to chase lightning bugs and put them in a jar. We always turned them loose, but it was fun to see how many we could catch. One night, a

lightning bug flew in Lila's eye and she went howling into
the house, by that time the bug was gone, but it scared
both of us. We stopped our bug chasing for awhile.

Beyond her house was a steep hill that we liked to
coast down in her little red wagon. The hill had been
graded down when the road was built below it, and the
constant passing of many feet had worn a smooth path on
top. Lila sat in front of the wagon and steered with the
wagon tongue. I sat in the back after I had given the wagon
a push to start us down hill. One day she lost control of
the wagon, and off that steep embankment we went to the

road below. It is a wonder we were not badly hurt, but aside from bruises and scratches, we were all right. We were afraid to tell our parents what happened for fear they would forbid our riding down the hill again, so we said we were running and fell down.

Lila's father raised a lot of wheat and every year the threshing machine came to their barn and threshed the grain. We decided to make a small thresh and used the seeded tops of grass for our wheat. Our thresh was made on a board, using nails, wire and empty spools (that thread came on), we rigged up something on the order of an old fashion washing machine ringer. By running the grass stems between the spools, the seeds were crushed and fell out— provided the grass was dry. We used pepper grass and a short stemmed grass with a fluffy head, but I do not know its name.

The Pool family had a large orchard where Lila and I liked to climb trees. We had spotted most of the bird nests in the orchard and were watching for the first baby birds to be hatched. Lila called me one morning to say the Jaybird family had some babies. I rushed down and we went to see the newly hatched birds. She climbed up first and announced all the eggs had hatched. Then it was my turn. Up I went, but just as I looked in the nest the mother bird returned. She flew at me with her wings spread wide, screeching as only a Bluejay can. I covered my head with my arms, but she pecked my hand with her beak. As she circled for another attack, I managed to get down from the tree. Lila and I took off as fast as we could go, with mama and papa bird right behind us—papa bird had heard the commotion and came to help. Those birds followed us to the house, and Lila's mother came out to see what was happening. She thought it was funny, and said that should teach us to leave baby birds alone. I had a scar on my hand for many years.

Lila was about two years older than I, and she soon reached the age when two years made a big difference, and we stopped playing together.

My next best friend was Eddie Belle Ross, whose father was cashier of the bank. She was younger than I, but we were about the same size. The bank joined our store, so she visited me almost every day. Eddie Belle's father liked to play tennis and so did my sister. She persuaded my father to have a tennis court built between the bank and our house. That tennis court added a new dimension to our lives. I learned to play, but was never great on sports, but I did like to watch the grownups play. That court brought a great deal of activity to our yard.

The Coming of Fall

I always had mixed feelings about the coming of fall and starting to school again. The weather was still warm and in the middle of the day it could be really hot. I remember one fall my mother made me two new dresses, and I thought they were just beautiful. One was pink voile with white flowers, it had long sleeves with a tight cuff. That year I sat in a back seat beside a window. The back of the school house was very high off the ground, and as I sat by that open window in the class room, so high off the ground, I imagined I was on a train on my way to some far away place. Dressed in my pink voile dress, with the cool breezes coming in the window, it was easy to day dream, and imagine all kinds of wonderful things.

The games we played at school were mainly town-ball and jumping rope. Town-ball was like softball with two exceptions: only girls played town-ball, and a wide bat was used with a homemade ball. The ball had a center of cloth rolled up, then covered with wool thread, and the outer cover was wrapping twine. It didn't bounce well, but it was a good strong ball and lasted a long time. I loved jumping rope, and could do all the fancy steps, but "hot peas" was my favorite. The rope was thrown as fast as the two rope throwers could move their arms. This kept one jumping at a very rapid pace, but it was fun. A count was kept to see how many times one could jump without missing. My sister was an expert at jumping rope, so I guess she taught me.

One thing I especially liked about fall was playing on bales of cotton next to the gin. Since my father bought cotton, there were sometimes 50 to 100 bales in the area. It was fun to jump from bale to bale without ever touching ground.

I liked going to the store and looking at all the new clothes and shoes that had come in. Choosing new clothes for winter required a great deal of thought. My mother seldom agreed with my choice in anything. Sometimes I won, but most of the time she had her way.

I looked forward to Halloween, because we usually had a carnival at school and a party at church.

I must have been in the third grade when my sister married. She had always been a "big baby" and when in college was constantly begging to come home. When she married she wanted her husband to go in business with my father and they lived in the house with us. They later bought the Maxwell house but never moved in, and later sold it. A new barn had just been built on the Maxwell lot, and immediately I thought of it as a new place to play. Since the Maxwell lot was behind our house it was easily accessible. The barn had a ratproof corn crib, with a wide sill that came up from the floor about three or four inches. We nailed a round pole across the door, and "skinned cats" on the pole. If you have never skinned a cat you have missed something great. You hang from the pole by your hands, swing your feet between your hands, and flip over onto your feet—almost like a somersault. We had to watch carefully so as not to hit that wide board that extended upward from the floor.

Addie Lou Giles, who lived about a mile from town, liked to come by after school and skin cats with us. Her mother had told her the afternoons were getting too short for her to visit me after school, but we found that if we rushed home instead of walking slowly, she would have time to stay a few minutes. One afternoon when she was flipping over, the pole broke and she hit her head on the wide board. We were literally scared to death, because she appeared to be unconscious, but she soon revived. She had a big knot on her head and it kept getting bigger. She didn't know what to do. She knew she would be punished for stopping by my house, if her mother found out, and the knot would surely show. She usually wore a knitted tam to school, so she decided she would wear her tam until the knot went down. I don't know what excuse she used at

home for wearing the tam, but I know she wore it at
school for several days, refusing to take it off. We did get
another pole but Addie Lou had lost interest in skinning
cats.

Winter Comes

There were always so many things to do before Christmas. I thought of winter beginning just as soon as Christ-
ms was over. Business was slow at the store after Christmas,
making it possible for my mother and sister to stay home
most of the time. There was a special joy attached to the
long winter evenings, for this was the time my mother,
sister and I sat before an open fire and read all the books
we had gotten for Christmas. We rushed through supper,
washed dishes, and brought the kitchen lamp to place beside the lamp already on the table in front of the fire.
Mother and sister took turn reading aloud. Thus I listened
to novels by Zane Grey, James Oliver Curwood, the Tarzan
books by Edgar Rice Burroughs, books by John Fox, Jr.
like *The Little Shepherd of Kingdom Come*, and *The Trail
of the Lonesome Pine*. There were books by Thomas
Dixon, *The Leopard's Spots*, and *The Clansman*. I got the
other side of the story, too, for I wept over *Uncle Tom's
Cabin*, and the stories of John Brown's escapades.

Then, of course, there was *Little Women, Little Men,
The Eight Cousins*, and *Jo's Boys, Tom Sawyer* and *Huck
Finn*. I loved The Five Little Peppers' stories, *Miss Minerva*
and *William Green Hill, Mrs. Wiggins of the Cabbage Patch,
Uncle Remus, Alice in Wonderland,* and *Peter Pan.*
Somehow I never cared about fairy tales. Our reading
sessions ended when my father came home from the store;
it was then bed time. However, he seldom came in before
eleven. Needless to say, early to bed and early to rise was
never practiced at our house.

Before leaving the subject of reading, I want to mention some of the magazines I knew. We took the *Woman's Home Companion*, I believe it later became the *Ladies Home Journal*, the *Delineator*, *The Youth's Companion*, and *Comfort*. This last one had household hints, and how-to articles, and I believe a few stories. *The Youth's Companion* was my favorite. It had children's stories, short stories and always one continued story. One series of stories, dealt with the life on the Old Squire's Farm near Portland, Maine. These were true stories and were later published in book form. There were three or four volumes. We ordered all of them when they were published, and I still have two volumes.

The Woman's Home Companion and *The Delineator* were my sources of paper dolls. *The Delineator*, especially, had pages of colored fashions for women which made lovely paper dolls. While we poured over these magazines

and books, my father read his two Atlanta papers that came in by train, and three or four county papers he felt he must read. He also took several farm papers as well as one or two political papers. We were really a reading family.

None of the children I played with were allowed to read novels, so I learned to keep quiet about the fact I heard novels read aloud. I don't know that I ever heard my mother say whether she approved or disapproved of children hearing adult stories. She may have had some doubts, but she and my sister loved to read so much, that they resorted to this means of entertaining me and getting me to do what they wanted at the same time. I would sit quietly just as long as someone read to me.

It was an interesting life growing up as I did, but the most important thing my family did for me, was teaching me to love books. I have always been grateful that no restrictions were placed upon my reading. In that way, I learned to be my own censor.

Chapter 8

TIED DOWN TO A GENERAL STORE

The store was "our living" and none of us thought of complaining about the many inconveniences attached to it. For instance, our meals were so irregular that we seldom ate as a family except on Sundays. During the week we ate in relays, because the store was kept open from early morning until late at night. Why the long hours? Our trade largely depended on farmers. They came to the store very early in the morning or late in the day, so as not to interfere with their working day. Frequently, they knocked on our front door at daybreak, and my father would get up and open the store for them. They did not think of this as an inconvenience, because we lived next door to the store and they felt every working man should be up at the crack of dawn.

In the evenings, after their day's work was over, farmers often came to town. They seemed to know when it was supper time at our house, and chose that time to come to the store. Spring and fall were the busiest seasons for farmers and for us.

There was another reason why the store stayed open late at night. My father was the "social type." The store was the gathering place for the men of the town. They came after supper to sit around the pot-bellied stove and talk. There they sat, exchanging local news, and discussing state and world news they read about in the daily papers. There was an excellent train service at that time, and the Atlanta papers came morning and evening, so the town people could get their papers at the local post office right after the trains came.

The "talking group" cleared out about 8:30 or 9 o'clock; they believed in an early bed time. The few left were the checker players. My father was an excellent checker player, and never tired of the game, but there were others equally as good. One player in particular, Lee Parks, walked one and a half miles to town to play. Many nights he and my father played until 12 o'clock, then he had the long walk home in the dark. Lanterns and later flashlights made walking at night easier and there was no traffic to worry about.

Keeping such late hours made the possibility of being awakened at dawn, by a demanding customer, not at all appealing. My father had a clerk to open the store between 7:30 and 8 o'clock each morning. So when he was not disturbed by an early customer, he had breakfast about 9 o'clock. We were all late sleepers—when it was possible. I suppose we had the only cow in the county, who frequently was not milked before nine o'clock.

The store carried all kinds of wearing apparel for the entire family and included a millinery department. We also had hardwear, groceries, and in an adjacent building was a warehouse where fertilizer and feed-stuffs were kept. Later a cotton gin was built. Business with the farmers was done on a credit basis. The merchant charged whatever the farmer needed during the year, and in the fall when crops were sold, he paid his bill. The merchant also did much of his buying on credit, paying his bills after the farmers had paid him. This system worked fine until the boll weevil came, and farmers were no longer able to pay their debts. Merchants who had given them credit were often bankrupt themselves, and some were forced to close their stores.

At home we had little need for real money. We had a large garden, we raised several hogs each year, had our own milk and butter, and our own chickens and eggs. Any other food we needed came from the store, as did our clothing. It was a simple and uncomplicated life.

The Spring Rush

Spring time was a busy season. Farmers had to buy fertilizer, seed, sometimes plows and tools. Work clothes were in demand. Flour and a few staple groceries were all the farmer needed to buy at this season of the year.

Just before Easter families came in to buy new clothes. Our millinery department was busy with women placing orders for their new Easter hats. All women and little girls wore hats. The milliner made up a few sample hats and had many pictures. Ladies, after looking at the samples and pictures, decided what shape, size and style hat they wanted, and their hat was made to order. The milliner's work was seasonal. The wholesale hat merchants had lists of milliners, and a merchant could make his own choice. We sometimes boarded the milliner at our house, but usually she stayed in another home in town. Many salsemen, then called drummers, came by train to towns carrying their sample cases, and might stay in a town for several days, so boarding houses were in demand.

After Easter business slowed down. Most of the early crops were planted, now it was time to do combat with grass and weeds. Cultivating the crops would keep all farmers busy until mid-summer.

My mother and sister were not needed at the store everyday, so we were busy with our own gardening. We hired someone to plow the garden, but we planted the seeds. Beans had to be planted on Good Friday, regardless of the weather. My mother's purpose in the early planting was to have fresh beans by Commencement Sunday at Perry-Rainey. We rented the railroad property in front of our house, so as to have more space for corn and sweet potatoes. At least three people were needed to set out sweet potato slips. One dug the hole, one dropped the slip, and the last covered the plant. Then came the watering. We used buckets and dippers to apply the necessary water to the newly set out potato plants. The barn well was just across the road, but many gallons of water had to be carried to give those plants as much water as my father said was needed for his precious plants. He did not care what we did with the garden, but he surpervised sweet potato planting. After watering, a hoe was used to pull dry soil to the plant. This helped to conserve the moisture and the plants did not dry out so fast—it served as a mulch. How I hated this job. We tried to have early potatoes to make potato pies to take to Campmeeting in Lawrenceville the third Sunday in August. Campmeeting was a big occasions—people came from miles around.

The camping part of the meeting began on Monday after the second Sunday, and preaching services were held twice each day by outstanding ministers. Small white cottages dotted the grove where the large arbor was built. Families owned the cottages and came each year for a week, it was a kind of vacation. Servants came along to do the cooking and look after the children. In the afternoons adults sat around under the trees talking and visiting with each other. The third Sunday was the grand finale. After morning service, small groups gathered and spread their lunches together, before going back for the afternoon service.

Summer, the Easiest Time of the Year.

My mother and sister were seldom needed at the store during the summer months, as business was "slow." We worked at home drying and canning fruit, canning vegetables, making jelly and preserves—and digging grass and weeds out of the garden.

The front of the store had a shelter over it, and in summer several benches and a number of cane-bottomed chairs served as a cool gathering place for loafers, who had nothing to do. Sometimes women also sat down to chat,

and checker games frequently took place. There were trees at each end of the shelter, and there always seemed to be a breeze.

Many people went to visit relatives and friends during the summer, but we never thought of closing the store. The only trips we made in summer were buying trips. My father sometimes went to New York and mother went with him on several occasions. But most buying was done in Atlanta. I was allowed to go with them to Atlanta a few times, but I found the trips tiresome.

Wonderful Fall

September brought a surge of activity. Box after box of new goods arrived at the store. My mother had to get the cook to come back, as she was needed full time at the store. We all worked at the store—even I could help unpack boxes, while others marked the cost and selling price on each article. Both the prices were coded. The cost was:

1 2 3   4   5   6   7   8   9 10

T.C. Flanigan and Vedie Elder were married by Jackson (Rev. Frank Jackson married them). The selling price code was:

1 2 3 4 5 6 7 8 9 10
F R I E D B A C O N.

The object of the codes was to give the clerk some leeway when dealing with customers who tried to get prices cut. This was called "dickering." Some people would never buy anything unless the price was cut. Clerks knew these people and automatically raised the price on everything shown them. Some customers would trade with only one person because they thought they got a better bargain from that particular clerk. My mother disliked waiting on a certain lady in town because she wanted every bolt of cloth taken down from the shelves before she could make up her mind what she wanted. I rather enjoyed the "table talk" after my family had a busy day at the store. Some of the dickering customers actually paid more than the retail price when they gave a clerk a hard time. Each member of the family had amusing experiences to tell.

After new goods had been marked, then came the job of "putting up stock." The shoes were on one side of the store, piece goods on the other. Men's hats were displayed in one front window, women's hats in the other. Beyond the shoe section there were shelves for men's hat boxes, underwear, socks and other things. Beyond piece goods were shelves for women's and children's underwear and

hose. Two aisles went down the center of the store, where glass showcases and counters were used for display.

At the rear of the store were groceries. Two rooms opened off the main store. One contained flour in bags and barrels, other staples and tools. The other room had women and children's dresses and the millinery department. Men's suits and coats were on round racks below the shoe department. We had a few dress forms on which to display dresses. I remember how pretty some of the dresses were and the handmade hats were gorgeous.

People flocked in as new fall goods were put on display. Sometimes our family would not get to eat the midday meal, which was our main meal, until mid-afternoon. Our cook usually stayed to prepare supper before leaving for the day, because my mother was too tired to cook when she came home.

My father hired someone to buy cotton, although he could grade cotton himself, he simply did not have the time. As farmers came to town to sell their cotton, they came into the store to settle their bills. Then the entire family came to town to be "out-fitted" in clothes for the winter. They might spend half a day, or an entire day in the store looking and buying. Such shopping tours really were hard on the clerks. A clerk was expected to give his undivided attention to that family until their needs were met, no matter how much time was required.

This fall rush was generally over by early November. We then planned special sale-days, and cut prices, so as to get rid of what we called "hard stock."

December brought Christmas preparations, and Christmas goods to be unpacked, marked, and put on display. I was in my glory, as I looked over the Christmas gifts. My Christmas toys were bought singly in Atlanta, so I saw no duplicates of what I would later receive.

The week before Christmas was literally a mad-house

experience. Breakfast was the only meal we could expect to be eaten in peace and quiet—and that had to be early. At night everyone was so tired by the time the store closed —about 11 o'clock—we simply fell into bed. Christmas Eve was the worst day of all. Last minute shoppers came searching for bargains. We did mark down all Christmas items late in the afternoon. Some country people came to the store after dark on Christmas Eve to buy "Santa Claus" for their children. Their purchases were simple things, but they spent a lot of time looking, knowing they were saving money by coming late. But this was the ONE night in the year we wanted to close early, in order to attend the Community Christmas Tree at one of the local churches.

Winter—Business Was Slow

We sold little during the cold winter months. My mother often sewed—she made most of my clothes. There was always mending to do. The weather seemed much colder than today, but of course, houses were poorly heated, and not as comfortable. We burned coal in our fireplaces, but with an open fire it is easy to roast in front and freeze in back. We burned wood in the kitchen stove and that room was always toasty warm.

In winter our family had more time together than at any other time of the year. In very cold weather my father might close early and come home. It was on such evenings the entire family played carom and popped corn over the fire. There was an art to popping corn over hot coals. It was so easy to burn it. I thought no one could pop corn as well as my father, and he loved being asked to take charge of the job. We usually had parched peanuts (in the hull) on the kitchen stove, and apples and oranges. These cold nights could be merry ones as we sat around the fire as a family group. Irons (flat irons) or bricks were sometimes heated before the fire and wrapped carefully to tuck away in beds to get them warm before going to bed.

It seemed that in winter my father and mother spent a lot of time looking over wholesale catalogues. Dishes and many odds-and-ends were ordered by mail. Anything glass came packed in barrels, and it was fun to feel down into excelsior and wonder what the next article would be. Mother and sister ordered many of our personal things from catalogues. Books were always ordered—trying to decide what books to buy was a hard job—we wanted all we didn't have!

Years later, two funny incidents came about through purchases made at our store, and merit repeating.

An Unusual Way to Decorate the Ceiling

The first two-quart size pressure cookers we had for sale, appealed to one of our local citizens. He looked at them every time he came to the store. Finally, my sister gave him a little sales talk, and assured him his wife would be delighted to have a small pressure cooker. He decided to take the cooker.

A few days later he was in the store, and my sister asked if they had tried the new pressure cooker. He seemded reluctant to answer, finally admitting they tried to cook some peas in it without reading the instructions, and filled it too full. The peas swelled, the safety gauge blew off, and a stream of peas shot all over the ceiling. He had to let them dry, then scrape the ceiling, and now he had come to town to buy paint to re-paint the ceiling!

Hot Biscuits

When packaged biscuits first came on the market, a man in town, whose wife was away on a visit, decided he was going to try those "store bought" biscuits. He came to the store and said he missed his wife's hot biscuits so much he had made up his mind to try the "store bought" kind.

He went home, got the oven nice and hot, placed the

round package of biscuits on the baking pan and put them in the oven. He left the room and a few minutes later he heard a loud explosion, and rushed to the kitchen. The package had exploded, blew the oven door open, and shot biscuit dough all around the kitchen!

He reported the incident the next time he was in the store, adding, "You know, I never thought about reading the directions."

Chapter 9

TOM-FOOLERY, EXPERIENCES IN A HOSPITAL WARD, AND NAME COLLECTING

I was in the third grade when my sister married. I loved my brother-in-law dearly, and life certainly changed after he joined the family. The store was my father's life, and he had little to do with what went on at home. Tom, was just the opposite; he was home-oriented. He liked working in the yard and garden, and could do any kind of repair work about the house. He whistled or sang when he worked. He screened in our back porch so we could eat there in summer. He re-landscaped our front yard, and

planted a lawn as well as new shrubbery, and put up a new
swing for me in the back yard. He liked to go swimming,
but of course we had no public swimming pools. At Park's
Mill there was a big pond formed by the overflow from the
dam, where people did swim and we went there. I had
never been swimming before. He was always ready to play
Parcheesi and card games with me. He played the violin
and sang well, as he had helped organize the first Glee
Club at Emory at Oxford. He did all these things in
addition to working at the store. I thought he was just
wonderful!

Tom and his brother, Loy Etheridge, along with Winfred and Mercer Pool, who were cousins, organized a quartet. Winfred called it the "Pools and Fools Quartet," and
if people could have heard all the funny stories told at their
practices, they would have thought it well named. Tom
and Loy had many unusual sayings that were not colloquialisms common to our community. They sometimes
used these expressions in public to embarrass their
respective wives, and thought it quite funny—but their
wives didn't.

Getting up from the breakfast table on Sunday morning, Tom would say, "Well, it's time to put on your *glad-
rags* and go to church." When I came out dressed in my
Sunday best he would say, "Ain't she *purt*, and she smells
like *gals goin'-to-meetin'*." I guess I did over indulge in
perfume sometimes.

Tom's Aunt Susie Ethridge, who was a staunch
member of the Methodist Church, walked as if she were
going to a fire. She was a sweet little woman, whose
favorite church song was, "Let the Lower Lights Be Burning," and she never missed a service, but when she walked
she almost ran. Tom would see her coming to church and
remark, "There goes Aunt Susie, *diggin' 'taters.*"

Biscuits were *sinkers* to Tom, and he did enjoy hot

biscuits with butter. He would come strolling in from the
store eating an orange, reach in his pocket and take out
another one, pitch it to me and say, "Have an *orangt*."

At night he'd say, "Guess it's time to *hit the hay*." In
the morning he would awaken me by putting his head in
the bedroom door shouting, *"Rise and shine."* When I
finally came out to breakfast he greeted me with the little
song, "Good morning, Mr. Zip, Zip, Zip, with your hair
cut just as short as mine."

He usually did the milking, and would announce as he
left for the barn, "I'm going to *juice the cow*." We had
pets of all kinds—cats, chickens, a big goose, and
sometimes stray dogs. Little baby chickens sometimes
became droopy and could not keep up with the mother
hen. Tom put them in a box at the barn and doctored
them. If one died he would report, "A baby chicken *kicked
the bucket* last night."

In summer, my mother often went to bed before the
rest of the family. When Tom came in from the store, he'd
say, "I hear Mrs. Flanigan *Sawin' gourds*, so I guess it's
time to hit the hay."

At meal time on weekends he was usually around when
food was placed on the table. He gave the call to a meal, in
one of three ways, *"Come and get it," "Soup's on,"* or
"Peas and cornbread again!" His voice could he heard all
over the house, and probably at our neighbor's as well.
Potatoes were always *"spuds,"* and if he was really enjoying
some special dish, he would say, "I guess you *suspicion* I
like this."

I had a fur-piece and muff that I wore only on special
occasions, because my mother wanted me to take "good
care" of it. On Sundays I would ask her, "Do you think I
should wear my furs?" If I did get to wear them Tom
would say, "My, I see you are wearing your *'fuzz'* today."

When the quartet was practicing for a performance

they often sang without the piano. Tom would say to my sister, *"Give us the key, Molly."* I knew where this expression came from. When my sister and Tom were growing up, singing schools were held during the summer. The purpose of a singing school was to teach children how to read music. The schools lasted about three weeks and were held at churches where song books were available for the teacher to use. Mr. Moore taught singing school in Auburn a number of times and his daughter, Molly, played the piano. When he wanted to get the right pitch for a certain key he would say, "Give us the key, Molly." These singing schools served a purpose. Most of the homes in town had either an organ or piano. After attending singing school children often wanted to take private music lessons, and parents usually agreed. There were a number of music teachers in town. My sister taught music for quite awhile.

Tom did not like the gospel music sung in some country churches—the kind that one keeps time to by tapping a foot, or gently swaying to the music. He called that *"Jay-bird music."*

Money was always *"ducketts"* to him. I was not aware of the literary origin of ducketts until much later. He might want to *"Mosey along,"* or *"hump-it,"* depending on whether he was in a hurry.

Our family adopted the use of Tom's "sayings," and still use them within the family. Our daughter and little granddaughter are familiar with them, so I suppose they will be passed down to future generations, as family colloquialisms.

Life in the Ward of a City Hospital

My sister was taken as an emergency case to an Atlanta Hospital. There was no private room to be had, so she was placed in a ward with 15 other women. She did not think she could stay in a ward, but found it so fascinating, she

later turned down a private room. While there she wrote
an account of her experience and read it to us when she
returned home. We found it both amusing and sad, and I
have never forgotten the people she described. This is part
of her account.

* * *

Fifteen pairs of eyes followed me as I was rolled down
the long room. Everything was perfectly quiet, but when
the curtains were drawn around my bed, life began again.
Laughter, the hum of conversation, music from a softly
tuned radio, the tinkle of ice in water pitchers—all this
floated through my curtains. I buried my face in my
pillow to smother my sobs of pain and anguish but, to my
surprise, I soon discovered that I was disturbing no one. I
became relaxed and the hub-bub around me was not as
nerve racking as I had feared. It was like the monotonous
buzz of bees flitting among flowers. No one cared parti-
cularly as to another's identity—they only wanted to
know, "What have you got, and who is your doctor?"
There was much sympathy and understanding in that long
room. When cries of pain or delirium were heard above the
general noise, not once did I hear anyone complain. It
was always a sympathetic, "Poor thing, I wish she could
feel better."

Life was so active around me I had, with curtains
drawn, almost the same privacy of a private room. Noise
and general activity prevented petty snooping. With curtains open one viewed a cosmopolitan area where the four
corners of the world had met, the rich, the poor, the edu-
cated, the uneducated, the good, the bad, and the indiffer-
ent. Yet, illness had brought all to a common level. I found
the ever-changing scene so fascinating, so full of friendli-
ness, pathos, tragedy, and continual excitement, that
when the nurse announced my private room was ready, I
surprised myself by saying,"I believe I'd rather stay here,

thank you." Later my husband could not believe his ears, when he learned I'd turned down a private room. I suppose I wanted to see how our "soap opera" would end!

The serial was being played before our eyes. The "heroine" was young and pretty, with a wardrobe suitable for a fashionable vacation spot. She had come to the hospital because her home doctor was an "old fogey" who could find nothing wrong with her. Her play for the hospital doctors and visiting men would have given a fiction writer many wonderful ideas. She was a star performer with costumes ranging from the loveliest negligees to the most revealing dresses. Her street clothes were eye catchers. She modeled according to her moods, and she modeled well. Since she was not sick, only under observation, she sometimes left the hospital to go to movies. Her husband's family discovered this, and she became the persecuted wife. The "audience" threw it's sympathy to the poor unsuspecting husband and two small children.

Turning from her to the sweet little old lady of some seventy-odd years, who fluttered over the room like a bird, was like turning from darkness to sunshine. She had a malignancy, but was always "getting better." She had never married, because after her parents died she had to take care of her brothers and sisters. But she hadn't missed much because they were like her own children, and now bless goodness, she had the sweetest grandchildren in the world. Her family lived at a distance, but when they came they showered her with love and affection. The way those "grandchildren" ran to her with open arms and cries of joy made me, too, decide that she hadn't missed much after all. She received more mail than any of us and practically every envelope contained money, mostly one dollar bills, but added together they gave her extra days in the hospital. Her church did not send flowers. "we are sending money for medicine," read the card. She was so deeply appreciative that we, too, rejoiced whenever another day in the hospital was made possible. Her three doctors stood near my bed listening to the renowned specialist who had been called to see her. When they walked away, plans for further medication had been made, with no cost to her. She could never understand how "The Good Lord" could stretch her money so far. The Golden Rule she had lived by worked two ways!

One of the most unforgettable characters was the young woman who radiated cheer so abundantly. Although in constant pain, she became known as our "shining star." Her clothes were brought nightly by her husband. "You see," she said with a smile, "I didn't have enough clothes to come to the hospital so everyone lends me things." Sometimes things were too tight or too big, but she never complained. Why should one ever hesitate to acknowledge having only a scanty supply of clothes when one is rich in friends who love enough to lend?

Constantly I watched the crippled-by-arthritis nurse, who lay helpless except for a few movements of her hands and arms. She asked no favors and seldom mentioned her condition. Her only relative lived in a distant state, and all her worldly possessions were in the trunk and bags around her bed. She never complained, but when you saw her helplessness and heard her crying in her sleep, night after night, your heart broke. She had been in the hospital eighteen weeks and was constantly growing worse. The insurance company was beginning to complain about the hospital bill. Her only luxury was the daily paper. Sunday was pay day for the paper she later explained to me, but I was startled my first Sunday morning there to see the newsboy taking her purse from one of her bags and opening it. But, instead of taking the money due him, he reached into his pocket and took out several coins which he dropped into the open purse. I wondered how long he had been doing this, for I had heard her say, when paying the maid for her laundry, "My little money is lasting longer than I thought possible." After replacing the purse the boy turned and glancing over the apparently sleeping people, he timidly and gently replaced the fallen sheet over the sleeping woman's bare legs. The tenderness and thoughtfulness of that newsboy was indeed a benediction!

There was the young woman who laughed and talked loudly and incessantly. At first we thought she was seeking attention in a coarse sort of way, but how wrong we were. The nurse had to help her walk and each day she became more and more helpless. Disease was destroying her before our very eyes. Her gaiety in the day seemed so pathetic, because at night in her sleep she would cry and scream, "No, no, don't let it happen to me." Then as though pleading with her husband she would say, "Don't hold me—let me kill myself before it happens to me." After that, even the most skeptical became tender and kind.

There were two women in the ward who had double-trouble, each had a husband facing serious surgery. One was a beautiful, mature woman whose clothes and luggage bespoke wealth. She lay day after day, silent except for much weeping. Early one morning she was wheeled away. "Where are they taking her?" echoed throughout the room. Then came the news, she was being taken to be near her husband—this was his operation day. Late that evening she returned, smiling, and announced, "The doctors say my husband will live. I'll get well now," and how rapidly she recovered.

The other woman whose husband was facing surgery was silent and cried a great deal except when her husband was brought to see her. Then she was cheerful and seemingly happy. At last the day came when her husband was to leave for a distant hospital and another cancer operation. The doctors had told her there was no hope for her husband, but he insisted on trying another operation. She dressed her prettiest, even donning jewelry, and left her bed to join the family party in the sunroom. She stopped by my bed, saying, "Pray that I may not break down and cry. I've got to let him go remembering me in smiles. I'm so doped-up I have little feeling. I told the doctors to help me through this day even if I have to go through hell tomorrow." She went with him to the elevator, waved and smiled as he was carried away, knowing that this was their last farewell. Staggering, she returned to the ward, and fell upon her bed unconscious.

But enough of the profiles of the occupants of the ward! Let's take a look at the lighter side of being in a ward. How do male visitors react when visiting a woman's ward? Some are frankly curious, enthralled by all that meets the eye, while others are greatly embarrassed. But soon, they too, become relaxed in the utter freedom of the room. To many who come alone, it requires lots of courage to enter, but how flattered one feels when some friend cares enough to be that brave. I noticed a man at the door of the ward. It was my husband's old college chum. He entered the door, glanced around, then stepped back into the hall. I thought he was going to leave. But no, he looked inside the room again, and clutching his hat in his hand and with face set straight ahead, he came down the long room to my bed. Laughing, I asked how he knew how to find me, because he didn't look at a single person. He gave a sigh of relief, "They said you were at the end of the room—and there's the wall," he answered. Visiting hours can be great occasions. I had my own loved ones, and my friends had theirs, but soon, as we knew each other better, it was like a family reunion.

To some, life in a hospital was luxury divine. One lady came to my bed to tell me goodbye. "Of course I'm glad to be well," she said, "but how I hate to leave this place. I never knew how wonderful it is to have my breakfast served in bed." She dabbed her tears as she went away, adding that she wished she had the money to stay a little longer!

Mealtime was a riot in the ward. It took me back to my college days, for here were the same old demands, the likes and dislikes. There was a hush of expectancy as the meal cart was wheeled in. Then came the usual comments: "That looks good," "I can't live on this little bit of food," "You always get the best looking tray, let's swap," "You'd think a person would get a little better service paying what we do," "O, such delicious meals," "Ugh, who said so," "Bring me some ice—and I mean right now," "Can't I have more bread?" "I want some more coffee—mine's cold." All this was followed by a calm as each settled down to enjoy her meal.

A ripple of delight always accompanied the arrival of a certain aide. She was neat as a pin, but not young. Her workworn face always carried a smile, and when she spoke one knew she had received few educational advantages. Everyone loved her, as she went from bed to bed smoothing covers, fluffing pillows, soothing a patient by saying, "Now honey, jes' be ca'm." She did the things the nurses did not have the time to do, and never seemed in a hurry. She stopped by my bed, and I learned she had wanted to be a nurse, but of course lacked the education, but she was grateful for the chance to work in the hospital so she could support her children. As she went her way down the room, the woman next to me said, "In as much as ye have done unto the least of these . . . ."

It was Sunday morning, and the fashionable young heroine of our "soap opera," declared we should have Sunday School. She would recite the books of the Bible; of course she failed miserably. Laughing, she said she used to know some church songs and wanted to sing, but the long forgotten words failed to come. The sweet little lady with the malignancy rose and walked slowly to the center of the room. All eyes rested upon her. Deep silence covered the room as she stood there repeating the Twenty-Third Psalm. "Now let us pray," she said. One by one voices joined hers in the Lord's Prayer. Afterwards, my neighbor mused, "I feel as if I'd seen a Rainbow." The arthritic nurse smiled and replied, "This room is filled with rainbows—for those who see."

* * *

Name Collecting

My sister had an unusual hobby of collecting names; she began this while still in the hospital and continued it for many years. The entire family became interested, and there was great excitement when one of us found a choice name.

What's In a Name?

When you are a collector of names there is a new world of enterainment to be found in: papers, magazines, directories, phone books, obituaries, social columns, road and store signs. Commonplace names, when combined as by marriage, can become picturesque oddities, humorous, and sometimes musical. They can be eagerly sought after treasures to the name collector.

What do you do with names? You organize them into groups and the results can be truly remarkable. A person's complete name, comprised of two or more words can, on its own merit, be astounding!

Peg Legg   Little-John Swims
Kitty Waits Long   Will Eddie Hoppe
Henry Will Fite   David Getz Better

Jerry Kums Tumlin
Grace Tooke Henry
Pansy Bugg
Jimmy Inoyou
C.U. Born
I. Ketchum
Tizza Goode Story
Ima Rose Bush
Jenny Bee Goode
C.A. Virgin
Sam B. Noble
3 Sykes brothers:
Dowell
Livewell
Diewell
Twins of a former
    Texas Governor
Ura Hogg & Ima Hogg
Darling Precious Child
Jim Garners Wheat
Andrew Betts Money
Donald Sells Wood
M.T. Bottle
Green Tree
Selecta Jury
Jessie Lines Panns
Jay Hazza Hobby
Shorter Sox
Hottern Hell
Kitty Katz
Fallen N. Love
Doris Loves Huggin
Hunter Brown Button
Rosey Brown Fudge
Heeza Luckie Guy
Icie Cole Waters

A. Jay Walker
John Knox Ball
Snow Flurry
Henry Butts Wall
Erna Dollar
C.U. Monday
Georgia Hills
Jesus Christ
Good Experience Wilson
A. Golden Locket
Lavender Pink Green
Etta Pickle
A. Wise Taylor
Christmas Angel
Merry Laughter

I.B. Weary
Miles Long
Windy Gale
Pink Head
Green Glass
Rusty Nails
Mark A. Line
Ima Sojourner
Shiver Ann Shake
Green Bean
Lisle Stocking
Green Apple Pye
Cole Coffee
Salmon Fish
Seldom Sober
Rusty Key
Rosey Pink Cheek
Washer Head
Jane Sells Coats
Ira Seams Moody

If parents would only think, when naming a child, how that name will sound to the general public, and the embarrassment the child will endure for a lifteime, I'm sure they would be more careful.

Organizing names into groups requires concentration and work as you try to decide on categories to use. I will give examples of categories and last names that fall under each category.

1. A peep into Noah's Ark: Animals: Catt, Hogg, Burro, Deer, Bear. Birds: Raven, Dove, Peacock, Lark, Robin. Fish: Perch, Bass, Trout, Salmon. Insect: Bugg, Bee, Wasp, Cricket, Roach.
2. *Combat*: Spear, Lance, Cannon, Warr, Armor, Trigger, Swords, Slay.
3. *End of Story*: Sorrow, Death, Coffin, Tombs, Graves, Bury, Dye.
4. *Dressmaking Items*: Folds, Stitch, Button, Binder, Brain, Felt, Leather, Lace.
5. *Wearing Apparel*: Capp, Hatt, Hood, Pants, Derby, Brogan, Stockings, Blouse.
6. *Direction*: North, South, East, West, Western, Westland, Northern, Southern.
7. *Distance*: Knots, Miles, Farr, Near, Furlong.
8. *Measures and Weights*: Gross, Gill, Pair, Pound, Peck, Barrel, Pints, Bottle.
9. *Special Days*: Holliday, Christmas, Easter, Valentine, Furlough.
10. *Months*: March, April, May, June, July, August.
11. *Seasons*: Spring, Summer, Fall, Winter.
12. *Days of Week*: Sunday, Monday, Tuesday, Thursday, Friday.

13. *Courtship*: Gurlie, Boye, Dates, Love, Loving, Darling, Dear, Huggin.
14. *Time*: Morrow, Week, Weekly, Daily, Night, Allday, Aday.
15. *Flowers*: Rose, Pansy, Lily, Thrift, Posey, Hawthorne, Fern, Daisy.
16. *Gardening*: Plant, Planter, Diggs, Hoeing, Spade, Trowell, Vine, Moss, Weed.
17. *Relatives*: Cousin, Kindred, Sisters, Brothers, Neese, Bride, Husband.
18. *People*: Mann, Menn, Persons, Bachelor, Widdowa, Nabors, Warwoman, Orphan.
19. *Childhood joys*: Toye, Doll, Horn, Kite, Ball, Bell, Batt, Gun, Arrow, Tops.
20. *Descriptive*: Bitter, Sly, Wise, Rude, Curlee, Vague, Crisp, Boney, Humble.
21. *Hardware*: Toole, Screws, Auger, Levell, Plane, File, Nails, Hammer, Bolts.
22. *Bldg. Material*: Wood, Stone, Marble, Brick, Blocks, Rocks, Plank, Slate.
23. *Parts of a House*: Roofs, Gable, Garrett, Walls, Eaves, Hall, Sills, Stairs.
24. *Objects in a home*: Bunk, Couch, Sofa, Clock, Plate, Cupp, Pitcher, China.
25. *Visit the Courts*: Burglar, Crymes, Gamble, Crook, Quarrels, Steele, Lawyer.
26. *Human Body*: Hair, Head, Brain, Chinn, Finger, Foote, Kidney, Heart, Bone.
27. *Medical terms*: Doctor, Payne, Hurt, Kutz, Burns, Boyles, Cough, Trimble.
28. *Action*: Tumblin, Canter, Hunt, Gallup, Dance, Jump, Swim, Rush, Hopp.
29. *Occupations*: Author, Preacher, Merchant, Singer, Baker, Miller, Shepherd.
30. *Royalty*: King, Earl, Sultan, Queen, Lord, Duke, Pope, Knight, Prince, Barron.

31. *Bible Names*: Adam, Eve, Eden, Moses, Cain, Luke, Salome, Lazarus, Solomon.
32. *Church Officials*: Steward, Deacon, Elder, Parsons, Nunn, Vicar, Prophet, Sexton.
33. *Trees*: Oakes, Chestnut, Holly, Birch, Sycamore, Beech, Ash, Poplar, Linden.
34. *Colors*: Red, Amber, Lavender, Jett, Pink, Brown, Black, White, Blue.
35. *Opposites*:

Long — Short	Slow — Swift
Bigg — Little	Bride — Husband
Goode — Badd	Topp — Bottom
Olde — Young	Gittens — Givens
High — Lowe	Few — Many
Large — Small	Farr — Near
Sweet — Sour	Dark — Light
Meek — Proud	Gladd — Moody
Rich — Poor	Joy — Sorrow
Jolly — Stern	Still — Lively
Sharp — Dull	Life — Death
Wide — Narrow	Born — Dye

The many names that end in "man" and "son" can fill pages. I have listed about half of the categories my sister, the late Mrs. Tom G. Ethridge, had in her five "Blue Horse" notebooks of names. A minister I knew, who was a popular after-dinner speaker, said his favorite speech was on the "Origin of Names." I heard him give this talk, and it was quite humorous, but not altogether flattering, as he developed the results of his research, revealing the relationship betwen occupations and names! But name collecting can be fun, and I recommend it—and it does not cost anything.

My brother-in-law used to tell of boarding with a Mr. and Mrs. Hogg when teaching in Richland, Georgia. There also was a Coffin family living in the town, and the Hogg family often commented that if their name was Coffin they would have it changed! It is no wonder that some people do want to change their name, but after getting used to the sound of one's own name it ceases to sound so bad—I suppose some early Hutchins raised rabbits (Hutch) for some feudal Lord, but I don't think of "rabbits" when I tell people my name. I think it sounds pretty good.

Chapter 10

THE EARLY DEPRESSION YEARS
PENNILESS BUT HAVING FUN

The Depression reached the cotton growers in the early
1920's. By 1925 my father was ruined financially. South
Georgia knew the destructive power of the boll weevil
first. This was before the day of crop rotation and cotton
was the farmer's one money crop. Farmers fought the
boll weevil manfully, gathering the punctured bolls by
hand and burning them. They tried putting poison in the
form of a powder on the plants. This was dusting. Later
this powder was mixed with a liquid, and they mopped

the plants, thinking this would stay on the cotton longer. Nothing they tried seemed to do any good. The boll weevil spread to all of Georiga.

At first, my father had men on the road selling poison. He obtained all the information available from the State and Federal Agricultural Departments, but they offered little help. Research had yet to be done on the boll weevil, so the farmer was relatively helpless in his fight against this new enemy.

Farmers could not pay their bills to the merchants who had furnished them seed and fertilizer, as well as food. The merchants were not able to pay their bills, and therefore were not extended credit to restock their stores.

Farmers next tried mortgaging their farms in order to get money to make a crop. Banks would lend money, but when notes were not paid they foreclosed on the mortgage and many farmers lost their land—and sometimes their homes. There was a movement away from the land, but jobs were hard to find.

This was the time when the farm WIFE began looking for a job and found it in the textile plants scattered over the state. Winder, 6 miles from Auburn, had several plants where overalls and work pants were made, and local women found jobs there. There was also a cotton mill in Winder. These women had never worked before, except in the field, and they found working conditions difficult. It was hard for them to master the machines, and get accustomed to "piece work" which required more speed and skill than most of them possessed at the beginning.

It was a blow to their husbands having their wives bringing in a pay check to meet family expenses from what they called "public work." Even though the money was used to feed and clothe the family so as to hold "body and soul" together, the women came to like the feeling of independence and coming home with a pay check. They had no desire to return to the role of farm wife, and they did not return! A new era had begun.

The men raised food for the family, and many of them began raising chickens. If a farmer could get a chicken house built, poultry companies were willing to place baby chicks on consignment and furnish food for the chickens. The farmer took care of the chickens, and when they were old enough for market he received a percentage of the profit. Some farmers succeeded in this new undertaking, others didn't. Many disliked the work—it wasn't farming— and they were farmers. But it was something to do, and they needed work.

What Merchants Did

The first thing my father did was close his bank and pay off the depositors. This took all the money he could get together. He was a stockholder in two banks in Winder, and one manufacturing plant. Many of his business friends were going into bankruptcy, and urged him to do the same. He would not even talk about it—to him bankruptcy was a disgrace. He lost his farm lands, the house and store were mortgaged to pay off the bank depositors and store debts. He could not restock the store, and he had nothing to sell, so the store was closed.

He was a good salesman. He was able to get work in Atlanta as a salesman, but it paid very little and he had to pay transportation on the train. My brother-in-law found work as a bookkeeper in Winder. What money was made went to pay the notes on the mortgage, in an effort to keep the house and store. The store was rented, since we could not use it.

We found ourselves "without everything" we had been accustomed to having at our finger tips. We ate mostly what we were able to raise at home, and eating habits were changed. We had no money for clothes, but did have

a few bolts of cloth left from the store, and my mother
and sister could sew, so we managed. The money the men
brought in went for essentials.

A former friend and lawyer in Atlanta, whose name
appropriately enough, was Banker, came to our rescue
many times in our effort to save our home and store. Had
it not been for him we would not have had a roof over
our heads.

These were trying times. My father had an intense
sense of family pride, and his spirit was crushed because of
his financial circumstances. The kind of financial world he
had known was crumbling around him. He did not have
the will to begin again and try to pick up the pieces. This
was true of many of his generation. The old system of
credit and "a man's word" being his bond was gone forever
—an era had passed for us, too.

We looked to my brother-in-law to make decisions for
the family. It was a struggle in adjustment for all of us. It
seems to me I grew up over night. I think I had been a
spoiled brat before the depression began its gradual
descent upon us. I certainly was unaccustomed to doing
without new clothes and a lot of things at Christmas. I
do not remember that I openly rebelled, but what I do
remember was a feeling of resignation and acceptance of
the situation. I never felt ashamed and resentful. My
mother and sister were bitter. My brother-in-law and I
assumed a quiet determination that did not waver.

The Fun We Had

All of this sounds as if we had a miserable life, but that
was far from true. Everyone in town was in the same pre-
dicament we were in. We still had church activities, singings, and many small get-together-meetings in our homes.
We invited people in at night to play Parcheesi, rook and
other games. We had popcorn and roasted peanuts to eat in

winter, because they were grown at home. We learned to make very economical cookies—with nuts from the trees in our yard added to them; we thought they were wonderful. We read more and had time to do things we had never been able to do before. Our yard had never been so pretty, as we now had time to grow and enjoy flowers.

I finished high school still having the bearest necessities. My high school graduation dress was made from a remnant of white taffeta left over from the store. I was home one year between high school and college because we could not afford college tuition. But I had so much fun that year I did not regret the delay.

There were three or four couples in town who formed what we called the Sewing Circle. We were together on weekends and sometimes during the week. Neither the boys nor girls had any money or jobs, but we found many ways to entertain ourselves, and were active in Sunday School and young people's organizations. I have never been any happier than I was that year. Staying busy doing useful jobs in the community gave a sense of satisfaction and fulfillment. The companionship with the boys and girls in the Sewing Circle was also rewarding. We did not feel sorry for ourselves because we lacked new clothes and other material things. We were content and happy.

I went to college on a so-called "shoestring," riding the local train back and forth to Emory each day. The train was discontinued, and the second and third year my mother, father and I lived in Atlanta. My father was still a salesman. I worked, part time, during my second and third year in school. My parents were not happy in Atlanta, and went back home in my senior year. I boarded in a private home, and was "paper grader" (known as student assistant) for Dr. Comer Woodward in the Sociology Department at Emory. This paid my tuition. Penny pinching had become a way of life for me, so I managed very well.

My clothes were mostly "made-over" from clothes that had belonged to my mother and sister in our more affluent days.

I had always resented being called the baby in the family, which to me implied being spoiled and petted. When I had an interview for my first job, after graduation, and handed over my freshly filled out application, I was elated over the comment made to me. I sat anxiously while the lady who interviewed me read my application. When she finished she looked up and said, "I would have thought you to be the oldest child in a large family of children." It was the greatest compliment Loretta Chappell could have paid me. I was forever grateful to her, because I felt at last I had overcome the reputation of being a spoiled brat. I give the Depression credit for maturing me beyond my years.

I am sure those of us who lived in small towns had a much easier time during the Depression than city dwellers. We had a place to live, a garden spot, chickens, and a cow. Water came from our own well; we could still use a kerosene lamp if need be; fuel would be our main problem. I feel I was fortunate to have been living in Auburn in those trying years.

I have a warm spot in my heart for little towns divided by railroad tracks. They offered so much to those of us who grew up there. They were once pretty, well kept, and prosperous. There were so many of them—and today they look deserted and forlorn.

City people seeking suburbia have bought land and built beautiful homes in little towns, but not where they can be seen from the highway that follows the railroad tracks. These homes are away from the noise of trains and the highway. No one seems to care how Main Street looks. A service station, a convenience store, a city hall, a post office, a school, a church, and perhaps a bank can be seen,

but where is the pride in the appearance of Main Street?
It is that deserted, nobody-cares look that haunts those of
us who have lived in a little town.

To The Little Towns of Georgia

I challenge the city officials and citizens of the railroad
    divided towns
To find ways to beautify those streets occupied by de-
    serted, dilapidated buildings, and piles of junk.
Make Main Street beautiful with the loving care little
    towns deserve.
Make them a living memorial to the town that once
    prospered because the Railroad came in the 1890's,
Bringing transporation and communication. The Rail-
    road was then the lifeblood of the little town.
Restore it, make it attractive for a new generation of
    people
Who seek happiness in the joys of Small Town living!